THIS DANCE IS
DOOMED

THIS DANCE IS DOOMED

Holly Kowitt

Feiwel and Friends • New York

A FEIWEL AND FRIENDS BOOK

An imprint of Macmillan Publishing Group, LLC
120 Broadway, New York, NY 10271

Our books may be purchased in bulk for promotional, educational, or business use.
Please contact your local bookseller or the Macmillan Corporate and Premium Sales
Department at (800) 221-7945 ext. 5442 or by email at
MacmillanSpecialMarkets@macmillan.com.

Library of Congress Control Number: 2019948800

ISBN 978-1-250-09135-2 (hardcover) / ISBN 978-1-250-09134-5 (ebook)

Book design by Trisha Previte

Feiwel and Friends logo designed by Filomena Tuosto

First edition, 2020

10 9 8 7 6 5 4 3 2 1

mackids.com

With Love to Arthur,
Mel, and Jean

THIS DANCE IS
DOOMED

Chapter 1

I watched in horror as my veggie tortilla roll-up flew through the air and exploded onto three eighth graders.

"AAAGGGGHHH!" they howled.

Everyone jumped up. The cafeteria "cool" table looked like a crime scene. Roxxi, a major eighth-grade diva, seemed to be dripping blood, which was actually salsa. Her perfect white shirt was trashed.

"You—you—" Roxxi pointed at me, sputtering. *"Sixth grader!"*

At James A. Garfield Middle School, it was about the worst thing you could call someone.

"DON'T YOU *DARE* INSTAGRAM THIS!" Roxxi warned the crowd.

People held up phones anyway. Roxxi and her friends—all Fashion Club members—gasped and wiped avocado goop off leggings, shirts, and boyfriend sweaters. I tried to help scoop up the wreckage.

←— Second-most-popular girl in school

How could I have been so stupid?

"I'm sorry," I mumbled. "*So* sorry!"

"She was EAVESDROPPING," Roxxi snarled as shredded lettuce fell from her hair.

"Ohhhh!" An outraged murmur spread through the group. I crawled under the table to scrape up black beans with my bare hands. "Who *is* she?" someone asked. The name Becca Birnbaum was unknown to them.

Roxxi swung her head under the table. "Get up here! I want to talk to you!"

Ugh. I sat on the bench. Roxxi stood over me.

"Listen, twerp," she said through gritted teeth. "What we say about prom is *none of your business.*"

I nodded, looking at the floor.

"Why do you care, anyway?" Roxxi's voice dripped with mock sweetness. "You think someone's going to ask *you*?"

The other girls broke into laughter. It was the funniest thing they'd ever heard.

They were right—I *had* been eavesdropping. But not for the reason they thought.

It had all started in the lunch line, which snaked around the cafeteria table claimed by the most popular eighth graders. The "cool" crowd. As I got closer, I overheard...

"She could get *anyone*."

"Why won't she tell?"

"Probably some jock, or—"

I smiled. They were dishing the new hot topic: Who was Sloan "Selfie" St. Clair taking to prom? She was the most drop-dead beautiful, glamorous girl in school. Everything about Selfie—her mansions, her boyfriends, her Swiss summer camp—was the subject of gossip. Apparently, she had some big-deal date lined up for prom, but no one knew who it was.

I half listened as the line moved along. Various cute guys were mentioned: soccer players, country clubbers. And then ...

"How about that guy Dinesh?"

My head snapped up.

"You know, the kid from India."

I leaned in farther.

Someone said something I couldn't hear. I moved over another inch.

WHOOOOOAA!

I lost my balance. My lunch tray flipped over, and the food went flying.

That's when everyone screamed.

Getting back to my usual lunch table was a huge relief. My best friends, Rosa Hadid and Preston "Prezbo" Bollinger, had seen the whole thing. They gave me support, sympathy, and half a sesame bagel.

"Just ignore 'em," Rosa said between pita bites. "Creeps."

"Even if you *were* eavesdropping . . ." Prezbo shrugged. "*So what?* It's not like you were releasing a deadly virus to destroy humanity. Or building an army of killer robots." He watched a lot of movies.

"What were they saying that was SO interesting?" Rosa asked slyly.

No way was I mentioning Dinesh.

I rolled my eyes. "Oh, you know. Prom stuff."

"Prom." Rosa made a face. "The word makes me want to barf. If I have to hear any more about Selfie's stupid date . . ." Rosa hated cheesy school activities and things that were too girlie. She preferred her souped-up bike, old army jacket, and flame-covered drum set.

Prezbo sucked on a chicken leg. "Prom's a joke."

"It's for morons," Rosa said.

They waited for me to trash prom, too.

Silence.

"Wait a minute . . ." Rosa moved closer, squinting at me. "Don't tell me you actually . . . *want to go?*"

My face felt hot. "I don't know."

"*Seriously?*" Prezbo turned to me, surprised.

I looked at the floor.

"You heard that talk about 'dates' and 'limos.'" Prezbo snorted. "That's not *you*."

Maybe I was a little tired of things that *were* "me"—Homework Club, allergy shots, all-girl birthday parties at the science museum. For once, I wanted to wear a fancy dress, borrow my mom's beaded evening bag, and dance with a boy.

"Forget it." Prezbo slapped my back. "Instead, the three of us'll do something awesome that night."

I didn't want to guess *what*.

"Deal?" He put up his palm. "Deal." Rosa high-fived him.

"Deal." I sighed.

Rosa nodded toward the "cool" table. "Those people are on another planet. You don't want to go to *their* party any more than they want to eat lunch with *us*."

Suddenly Prezbo froze. "Ahem," he said. Rosa looked up, and her jaw dropped. I turned around.

Selfie St. Clair, eighth-grade glamour queen, was standing there.

Chapter 2

$\mathcal{M}$y stomach fluttered as Selfie whisked me to a less crowded corner of the lunchroom. We sat down at an empty table. "I need to talk to you," she said.

People stared. The tall, beautiful blonde and the short, plain redhead didn't belong together. Selfie was the most popular girl in town. Everyone knew the stories: Her mansion had its own movie theater. She once flew to Paris just to get her hair cut. She had multiple boyfriends, all in high school.

And I was ... well, me.

"Sounds like I just missed your epic spill." Selfie's eyes were sympathetic. *"So sorry!* I slammed Roxxi

— product-free hair
— freckles
— free T-shirt
— lucky rabbit's foot

The BABYSITTING BUNCH

for going ballistic on you." She leaned over and hugged me. "That is so *not okay*."

"Oh, uh, thanks," I said, thrilled and embarrassed.

"I wish I'd been there to help," Selfie said. "But my personal shopper was showing me this ultra-fierce dress." She pointed to my top. "Sick shirt, by the way. Yellow is the new denim."

Selfie wasn't like anyone else I knew—in fact, we were total opposites. We'd met by accident when I hit her with a volleyball and broke her arm. Injuring the most popular girl in school had pretty much meant my life was over. So I'd tried to make it up to her, and we ended up having a terrifying adventure that nearly got us kicked out of school. The big surprise? How nice she was. We'd texted for a while, and I'd helped her out of some minor disasters. But that was weeks ago, and I hadn't seen her since, except for a few waves in the hall.

I couldn't imagine why she needed to talk.

"So who's your big mystery date?" I dared. "The whole school's talking about it."

Selfie stopped and waved at people, like a beauty queen at a parade. A guy in a football shirt high-fived her. She blew someone a kiss. Then she leaned over and whispered sharply.

"I don't have one."

WHAT?

"You don't have a—"

"SHHHHHHH!" She looked around. "No one knows."

Why is she telling me? I wondered.

Her voice dropped to a whisper. "This is *serious*. If anyone finds out?" She shut her eyes. "I'm dead."

"Aw, Selfie—" I started to protest.

"I didn't mean to lie," she said sadly. "People kept asking who I was going with—I had to say *something*. Someone would turn up, I figured. No one did. Now I'm trapped. Oh, Becca!" Tears sprang to her eyes. "Can you get me out of this?"

"ME?" I froze.

"Yes." Selfie sniffed. "You have to find me a date."

"A . . . *date*?" I laughed, not sure I'd heard right.

She bent her head. "Or else I'm ruined . . . humiliated . . ."

Holy crud.

"Selfie . . ." My heart was pounding. "You know I'm a sixth grader, right? Most of the time I'm reading, studying, or drawing posters for Debate-A-Palooza. *I don't know guys.* How do you think—"

Selfie raised her hand, dismissing my worries. "It's not so hard! It could legit be *anyone*."

"Anyone?" I raised an eyebrow.

"Totally!" She shrugged. "Long as he's really handsome and supercool."

I thought about the guys I knew.

I rubbed my temples, still in shock. "What kind of prom night are you picturing?"

She sat up straighter.

"Well . . ." Her face lit up. "It starts with a great promposal. Like putting it on a Jumbotron at the football stadium. Spelling it out with cupcakes on your driveway. *Whatever.*"

I was fascinated. "Keep going."

"He picks me up in a horse-drawn carriage or stretch limo with PlayStations."

Geez. "That sounds—"

"The after-party doesn't have to be *insane,*" she insisted. "I like that restaurant with the three-story waterfall. Or a midnight cruise."

I whistled.

"It's great to have dreams," I said. "But, Selfie, this is *middle school.* You have to be realistic. I mean, I'd like to dance with Dinesh O'Reilly!" I joked, trying to be outrageous. "But *that's* not going to happen."

Selfie's eyes widened when I said "Dinesh."

"Becca, I *need* you." Selfie's eyes were pleading. "Obvi, I can't tell any of my other friends about this."

The most popular girl in school is begging me!

My head was spinning. I imagined us hanging out at her place.

No! I had to face facts: I couldn't do anything for Selfie, even though I really liked her.

"Selfie, I . . . I wish I could help!" And I meant it. "But I couldn't find an eighth grader a date *if my life depended on it.*"

It hurt to see her eyes mist up again. But I knew I'd done the right thing.

Chapter 3

The next day, Selfie was waiting at my locker.

"Just LISTEN," she said before I opened my mouth. She pulled me into a private huddle. Was she still hoping I'd find her a prom date? That was *so* not happening.

"I have an offer for you," she said.

I sighed.

"If you find me a prom date?" Her voice was low and urgent. "I'll get you a dance with Dinesh at prom."

WHAT? My heart leaped.

"I just got some intel," Selfie confided in a sly

← wild hair

← bike helmet

"Woke" T-shirt

rawhide wrist cord

voice. "Dinesh is unattached, and—*sort of*—knows who you are."

My stomach lurched.

"Y-you TALKED to him about me?"

The thought was horrifying. *Of course* he didn't know who I was! Sixth-grade nobodies were invisible to cool seventh-grade guys. Dinesh was a cute transfer student from India with wild black hair and a crooked smile. He wore unlaced hiking boots, and a red bandanna swung from his backpack. Since he'd arrived at

Garfield two months ago, he'd been my secret crush.

Not that I'd ever *spoken* to the guy. I'd only sneaked peeks of him in the halls, recycling room, and graphic novel section of the library.

"Sure, we talked." Selfie shrugged. "It was NBD."

I freaked out. "DON'T DO ANYTHING ELSE!" I grabbed her arm. "You might have already ruined—"

"Becca?" Selfie smiled. "I *got* this."

My heart was still pounding.

"Your dance with Dinesh?" Selfie nodded. "I'll make it happen. I can also get you a free prom ticket if you help me on the Dance Committee. I'll lend you a killer dress. You're going to totally *crush* it."

A free ticket? A killer dress? A dance with Dinesh?

My brain was overwhelmed. "But I said I'd do something with Rosa and Prezbo that night!"

"And miss the best party at school, ever?" Selfie gasped. "It's going to be NEXT LEVEL."

But—but—

Wouldn't it feel wrong not to be with Rosa and Prezbo? We'd made a deal. Didn't I belong with them?

I knew what I SHOULD say.

"Selfie, I hope you find someone great, because you deserve it. People don't realize how nice you are. And the thought of dancing with Dinesh is beyond thrilling. But I still don't know how to find you a 'really handsome and supercool' date. So I'm going to have to turn down your amazing..."

But somehow, I couldn't say it. I wanted to go to prom. Maybe I could help Selfie, somehow. Rosa and Prezbo would understand. And the chance to dance with Dinesh was a freakish, one-time possibility.

My resistance weakened.

"Please," she said quietly. "Becca, I really need you."

I hesitated.

"Okay," I burst out. "Yes!"

Why not?

"WOOOOOO-

HOOOOOO!" She jumped up and punched at the ceiling. People stared at her little happy dance around the hall.

We laughed and bumped fists and fluttered our fingers in a wacky handshake.

"You won't be sorry!" Selfie said.

I'd probably end up regretting it. But for one crazy moment, I was in heaven.

When Selfie and I walked into the Dance Committee meeting together, everyone's eyebrows shot up.

"What's she doing here?" Roxxi frowned. The classroom was filled with Selfie's friends: D'Nise Cousins, Roxxi Barron, Margaux Frost, Vivienne Ling, and Chaz Green, a guy who hung with the girls, and a few others. They were crowded around a table, watching a YouTube video on a laptop.

"Becca's my new assistant," Selfie announced. I nodded and slipped into the seat next to her.

"W-What?" Roxxi sputtered. "You can't just go appointing random sixth graders—"

"She's not 'random,'" Selfie corrected. "She's a

student council-whatever-it-is and went to, like, biology camp. Her screen saver is of famous women librarians, or folk singers, or something...."

Her mangled sales pitch wasn't doing me any favors.

"Um, Selfie?" I tugged her sleeve.

"And besides..." Selfie lifted her chin. "She's my friend."

I felt a flush of pride.

Roxxi sighed loudly. D'Nise looked alarmed. Chaz and Margaux seemed to be stifling giggles.

"Well, then, *I'm* getting an assistant, too," Roxxi announced. She and Selfie always competed with each other—over boys, parties, Instagrams, the "Golden Handbag" Award at Fashion Club. Some people thought they were the same type, but I knew the difference. Selfie had a heart.

"What*ever*." Vivienne winked at me. She was one

JAXON & KAYLA: RUMORS FLY

of the nicer ones, quieter than the others. "Hi, guys. We were just watching Clem's latest post." Everyone turned back to the screen. Clementine Ferrarra, an eighth grader I'd seen around school, was saying, "What tall redhead is going with what ripped jock? Tune in tomorrow!"

"She made her own YouTube channel," explained Vivienne. The sign behind Clementine said: HARD-HITTING PROM NEWS—AS IT HAPPENS!

"She broke the story of Brooklyn Rossiter and Dre Landers," said Margaux. "That was huge."

A prom news channel—*just for our school?* I was starting to get what a big deal this was.

Clem signed off, and Roxxi shut the laptop. "We've got a thousand things to do," she said. "Branding. Marketing. Outreach. How do we get the latest state-of-the-art prom technology?"

"For sure."

"*Totally.*"

People nodded.

Wow. It felt like a meeting at Google, NASA, or the Pentagon.

"But first, we have something BIGGER to discuss. . . ." Roxxi lowered her voice, building suspense.

Everyone leaned in.

"*Who's* going with *who*?" Roxxi had a wicked gleam in her eye.

Everyone laughed except Selfie, whose face went pale. But a second later, she'd rebooted with a fireproof smile.

"Ashleigh's going with Mason," Margaux volunteered.

"Shut UP!" Ashleigh pretended to get mad. "Well, you're going with Bennett."

"Only if he promises to shave." Margaux smiled, letting us know he was older.

As more dates were revealed, Roxxi stayed strangely silent. Someone finally asked . . .

"How 'bout you, Roxx?"

"Who, *me*?" Roxxi said a little too quickly, and I

realized the whole conversation had been a setup. You didn't brag about your date; you made others drag it out of you. "He's a freshman at Glen Lake," she announced sweetly. "You don't know him."

Then she looked at Selfie. "Your turn."

"Selfie won't tell," D'Nise announced.

"Oh yeah?" Everyone turned to the Queen Bee.

Selfie laughed. "I can't."

"C'mon, *spill!*" D'Nise begged. "You and Mystery Man have to double with us."

Selfie pantomimed zipping her mouth shut.

"Mason Dennehy!" "Vernon Katz?" "Forrest Takada!" people guessed.

"Oooh, sorry." Selfie bit her lip, like she was *dying* to tell but couldn't. I was the only one who knew she *did* have a secret—just not the one they thought.

"Is it the quarterback—what's his name—from Ridgewood?"

"The Italian prince from Swiss summer camp?"

" . . . the mayor's son?"

Roxxi's eyes flashed as she lost control of the discussion. Finally, she slapped her pink phone on the table like a judge's gavel.

"PEOPLE!!! FOCUSSSSS!!!!!" she blared.

Everyone shut up.

D'Nise wagged her finger at Selfie. "Okay, but next meeting we want name, address, yacht size. Don't hold out on us."

Selfie gave an adorable shrug and took out a pen with a pink feather on it. I wondered if anyone but me saw her hand shake.

Chapter 4

"Prezbo, do you know any eighth-grade guys?" I tried to sound extra casual. We were at Heroes & Superheroes, the sandwich shop/comics store. I was hoping he'd be too distracted to wonder why I was asking. "Or do you know where they hang out?"

"Why?" Prezbo didn't look up.

"Just, you know . . ." I couldn't spill Selfie's secret. "Wondering."

"I know a few. From *Action News*." That was our school TV show, where Prezbo did video game reviews.

"Oh yeah?" I tried not to sound too interested.

He turned a page.

"Are any of them, uh, nice?"

"I don't *know*." Prezbo sounded irritated. "Some are okay. Some are dirtbags."

I tried a more direct approach. "Do any of them talk about . . ." I hesitated. "Prom? Who they're going with?"

"PROM?!" he exploded, like it was the world's stupidest question. "Why?"

"Forget it," I said quickly.

"You're still thinking about *that*? We already decided." He went back to his comic book. "Let it go."

I knew I had to tell him.

"Well, see, uh . . ." I swallowed. "Selfie offered me a

free ticket to prom if I'd help her on the Dance Committee." No need to mention the dance with Dinesh.

Prezbo kept reading.

"So? You told her you had plans, right?"

"*Yeah*, but . . ." I looked at the floor.

Prezbo put down his comic book. "Oh *no*." He scoffed. "You've got to be kidding."

He looked at me like I was a traitor.

"Listen, Prez." I swallowed again. "I-I want to check it out. It'll feel weird not to be together that night, but if I don't go, I might feel like I missed something."

Prezbo was so startled that he leaned on a rack,

and a bunch of comics tumbled to the floor. The noise made the store clerk look up, a shaggy-haired guy with a headphone in one ear. "Hey, man," he rasped. "You barf on it, you bought it."

Prezbo scowled and stooped to pick up the fallen comics. "We made a *deal*," he muttered to me.

"I'm sorry, Prez," I pleaded. "But some things are too good to pass up! I mean, if you had the chance to film your zombie drag-race movie for the Horror Network that night? I'd say, *go for it*."

He sniffed. "There isn't a 'Horror Network.'"

"*Whatever*." I shrugged. "Sometimes we just like different things. That's okay, isn't it?"

"Prom's just a bunch of girls arguing about stupid decorations." Prezbo scowled. *I expected more from you*, his eyes said.

We stood there awkwardly at the comic rack.

"You know, prom isn't ... it's not as bad as you think," I said. "It's about the school coming together, not just ..." My phone rang. It was Selfie.

"Listen," I whispered into the phone, turning away from Prezbo. "I'm actually kind of—what? I don't *know* how many silk flowers for the Venetian gondola." I tried to lower my voice. "*Who*'s being a promzilla?"

When the call ended, I was scared to meet Prezbo's eyes. He shook his head.

"Dave's Diner, rear table, around four thirty," he said, resigned.

I looked at him blankly.

"*That's* where eighth-grade guys hang out."

"Oh, Prezbo! You're the greatest!" I squeezed his arm excitedly. "I asked because of Selfie. I can't tell you why, it's a long story—"

He sighed. "It always is."

· · ● · ·

I heard them before I saw them.

"Suck it, Feldman!"

"OOOF!"

" . . . Cratered in the last quarter—"

"FREAK!"

"Putting up decent numbers, but—"

Seeing the school's "coolest" eighth-grade jocks talking loud, laughing, and shoveling down food at the diner made me groan. No way could I walk over there and pretend to interview them for the school paper. *Not even for Selfie.*

I turned around to leave.

But before I could, eighth grader Tripp Nolan blocked my way. He was holding a tray of foot-long hot dogs.

"Coming or going?" he grunted.

"Um . . ."

I thought of Selfie begging me to help her: *Becca, I really need you.* How she'd told everyone at the meeting, *She's my friend.*

Deep breath.

"Actually, I'm—" *Here I go.* "I'm writing a story for the *Gazette*!" I yelled. Dave's Diner was as loud as a rock concert. "Could I ask you and your friends some questions?"

He shrugged and motioned for me to follow . . .

Although the guys stuffed into the booth didn't know me, I certainly knew who *they* were: Jonah Belasco, "Six-Pack" Feldman, Elijah Wu, Tyreese Dobbs, and Zach Pirotta.

Tripp led me to their table, and I stood there awkwardly. "She wants to interview you losers," Tripp explained. Jonah and Elijah didn't look up from their phones. Tyreese continued squeezing ketchup on each individual french fry. Six-Pack chugged a jumbo soda, then gave an enormous foghorn-like *BUUUURRRRRP*.

"Man—" Jonah shook his head. "That is *so* rude." Then *he* belched, and everyone laughed.

Tripp pushed Six-Pack to make room for me. Six-Pack shoved him back, and then everyone started shoving one another. Finally, the group slid sideways, and I wedged into a spot at the end. I took out my notebook and a pen.

"Thanks," I said. "I just have a quick question about . . . prom?"

All talking instantly stopped.

Talk about a conversation killer. The only sound was the wheezing of Tyreese's ketchup bottle.

"Is anyone, uh, planning to go?" I tried again.

Shrugs, sighs, grunts. I felt like a detective questioning gang members who'd agreed not to snitch.

"Are you looking *forward* to it?" My voice was high and nervous.

Instantly, I knew it was the World's Dumbest Question.

CRUD! How had I messed this up so badly? "Sorry. At the girls' table, they won't *shut up* about this."

I saw a flicker of something on their faces—interest? Irritation? Finally, Tyreese spoke.

"No, man, we're into it." He sighed and put down the ketchup bottle. "But limos and flowers? Then a *restaurant*? How much money you think I *got*?"

Then the dam broke.

"They want you to rent a tux—" Jonah's voice cracked.

"Buy a corsage—" Elijah interrupted.

"Tickets are fifty bucks!" Tripp howled.

"And you can't just *ask* 'em," Jonah muttered.

"*Nuh*-uh! You have to write it on a pizza with green peppers. Or fill up her locker with balloons."

"It's out of control!" Elijah pounded the table.

Wow. They had *plenty* to say about prom.

"I overheard Selfie talking about a horse-drawn carriage?" Six-Pack shook his head. "I was like, *no way*. What guy's going to do all that?"

I grabbed the opening.

"I think a lot of guys would be happy to take Selfie to prom." My lips curled into a sly smile.

The table went quiet again.

"She doesn't go out with eighth graders," Tripp said flatly.

Zach tossed a fry in the air and caught it in his mouth. "Probably has some high school guy."

"Or dude from England." Tyreese nodded.

"Who drives a Ferrari," added Six-Pack.

"With a monster sound system—"

"When he's not heli-skiing!"

"You guys are wrong." I leaned in. "Selfie goes out with guys her age. *Totally.*"

The guys exchanged glances that said, *Riiiiiiight.*

Elijah talked around a mouthful of fries. "Shee'sh out of our league. Way, *way* out."

"Selfie's kinda scary," Zach said between hot dog gulps. "No thanks."

They were terrified? These were the most popular guys at school!

But—but—

"But she's so beautiful!" I burst out. That's me—always sticking up for the poor, unappreciated super-gorgeous.

"Yeah, but . . ." Tyreese shook his head. "A real babe like that? It's—"

"Too much pressure," Zach finished.

More nods and grunts.

"Thing is . . . ?" Jonah leaned forward and lowered his voice. *"We don't know what we're doing."*

It was an amazing admission from one of the school's biggest jocks. I thought about him rolling through the halls in soccer gear, surrounded by beautiful girls.

"Someone like Selfie?" Six-Pack said. "You can't take her to your usual places."

"She'd want you to be..." Mason hesitated. "Older."

"Richer," added Tripp.

"Cooler."

Wow. I'd always felt jealous of the Fashion Club crowd—but maybe their efforts weren't having the intended effect. If guys were too intimidated by them, what good were their expensive clothes and makeup?

This was bad news for Selfie.

"Hey, uh—" Tripp snapped his fingers at me. Of course he didn't know my name. "*What'd* you say this newspaper article was about?"

The guys all turned toward me.

The *newspaper article*! I'd been so busy trying to crack the code, I'd forgotten my alibi. It was time to get out of there.

"Standard newspaper story." I closed my notebook and stood up. "Thoughts on prom. The middle school food chain. Shattered dreams. Unintended consequences. The human condition . . ."

"Huh?" Six-Pack blinked.

"Thanks!" I said, bolting out the door.

Chapter 5

The next day, I realized I needed more intel. Which eighth-grade guys didn't have prom dates yet? If only there was someone who knew ...

"Welcome to my *insane* life," said Clementine, who had the prom news/gossip show on YouTube. I'd gotten her number from Selfie, and twenty minutes later, I was at her door. She wore a side ponytail, an oversized tee, and slippers shaped like panda bears. A dry-erase marker drooped from her mouth like a cigarette. She looked bleary, like a student up all night cramming for final exams.

"Prom's only two weeks away, so I'm, like, *fried*.

I'm basically living on cake pops and Vitaminwater."

We entered her bedroom. I recognized the silk striped couch and fancy bed from her show.

"What'd you say your name was?" Clementine asked. Before I could answer, a Beyoncé song drowned me out. She dived for her phone.

"Yeah?" Clementine grabbed her notebook, a busy reporter on deadline. "Tanner and Riley . . . is that a definite?"

While she talked, I checked out her whiteboard.

The call ended. Clementine sank into the couch and patted the spot next to her. I sat down. *"So . . ."* She leaned in. "You got a scoop?"

"A scoop?" I shook my head. "I don't—"

"BFFs not speaking?" Clementine's eyes lit up. "Double-crossings? Backstabbings?"

Whoa! "No, actually—"

"Date stealing? Mall brawls? Freak-outs?"

"Wait—"

"Butt dialings? Meltdowns?" she begged.

"Clementine!" I interrupted. *"I don't have any gossip."*

Her shoulders slumped.

"I'm doing research. For the Dance Committee," I went on, trying to sound matter-of-fact. "I just wanted to know which cute, popular, eighth-grade guys don't have prom dates yet."

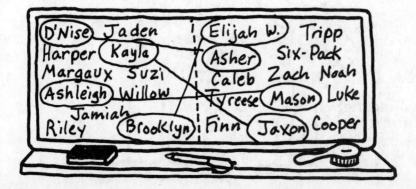

Clementine frowned as she took in my babyish ice-cream tee, flat chest, and no-name sneakers. "Um, no offense? But maybe you should think about . . ." She cleared her throat. "Guys your own age."

I laughed. She thought I was asking for *myself*?

"No, no, this isn't for *me*! It's for the Dance Committee." I put on my student council voice. "We just, you know, wanted to check the numbers. . . ."

She rubbed her chin.

"*Now* I recognize you!"
She slapped her forehead.
"You're, like, Selfie's helper
or something!"

I nodded.

"Oh wow. This is about
Selfie, isn't it?" she said slowly.

"*What?*"

"Selfie hasn't got a date!" Clementine jumped up
like she'd won a game show. "SELFIE HASN'T GOT
A DATE!"

Holy crud. I'd just leaked Selfie's most humiliating
secret—to a professional gossip.

"No way!" I tried to sound calm and amused, even
as my brain was exploding.

"*That's* why she wouldn't tell—"

"SELFIE'S GOT A *VERY* COOL DATE LINED
UP," I blurted.

Clementine hurled herself back on the couch, her
eyes glued to mine. She wasn't sure which piece of
hot gossip to believe—that Selfie didn't have a date or
that she had a great one.

She poked my chest. "*Spill.*"

CRUD!

"It's somebody—really good." *Every second I just get in deeper.* "I can't tell you who, but he's, uh, he's *major.*"

She leaned closer. "Why should I believe you? If Selfie has a hot date, why do you need the names of unattached eighth-grade guys?"

My mouth went dry. I could think of only one way out.

"Okay, I admit it," I lied, chuckling. "Those names *were* for me. *I'm* the one looking for a date. You were right."

She looked doubtful.

"I know," I continued, shaking my head. "It's not every sixth grader who'd aim for the most popular jocks. . . ."

Her eyes said, *That's for sure.*

"They only *think* they want beautiful, developed, eighth-grade girls," I confided. "What they *really* want is someone good at word games."

She stared at me like I was psycho.

Good. Better to be known as the Crazy Sixth Grader than to leak Selfie's secret.

"Uh-huh," she said, backing away. "Right."

"If those guys just got to know me . . ."

By now, Clementine was halfway across the room. She pointed at the dry-erase board as if to say, *It's all yours.* With a sigh of relief, I copied down the list of unattached eighth-grade jocks.

· · ● · ·

My mom squinted, looking out our living room window. "Honey? Why is there a nineteenth-century Austrian general in the driveway?"

I ran to the door and saw a guy in a military-looking costume. It took me a minute to realize he was Selfie's chauffeur.

"I'm Reinhardt, Miss St. Claire's driver," he explained. "She's waiting in the car to take you to school."

"What?" My mom gave me a sharp look.

I dived for my backpack and pulled a jacket out of the closet. "It's a long story," I told her. "My new friend—"

Reinhardt went back to the car, and Selfie appeared at the door. She was wearing her rock-star-at-the-airport look: trench coat hastily thrown over leggings, three-inch heels, sunglasses, hair in a glamorously messy topknot, tumbler of coffee clutched in her hand. She looked about twenty-five.

"Becca?" My mom's voice held a warning.

"Hi, we haven't met." Selfie held a manicured hand out to my mother, who was shorter than her. "I'm Sloan St. Claire."

"How do you two know each other?" My mom's eyes traveled downward, taking in Selfie's diamond ankle bracelet and quilted Chanel purse. I could tell she knew the answer wasn't "debate team."

"She's—we're—" I stammered. This wasn't the time to explain how we'd lost the principal's bra together and almost got kicked out of school.

"Becca's my assistant on the Dance Committee." Selfie's voice was smooth. She knew how to talk to adults.

"I see." Another detail I "forgot" to mention. My mom looked hurt.

Selfie turned to me. "Sorry, I should've texted. I'm dying to know how it went with those jocks."

Now my mom looked truly alarmed.

"Alone with six guys, you must've gotten *something*." Selfie frowned and flicked a granola cluster off my shirt. "Were they *all* eighth graders?"

My mom's eyes got even wider. "Becca?"

"It was a group interview! For the school newspaper." I sighed and turned to Selfie. "My mom's getting worried...."

"Oh no!" Selfie reached down and patted my mom's shoulder, anxious to reassure her. "Everything's cool.

It's not like she was playing Seven Minutes in Heaven at some guy's party while his parents were in Turks and Caicos."

"*WHAT?*" my mom croaked.

Oh, crud.

"Let's *gooooo.*" Selfie tugged my sleeve. "Before the principal freaks out on us again."

I could see my mom's brain spinning furiously as she tried to sort out a blitz of new information: I had contact with older boys, trouble in school, and some very weird new friends.

"Sloan." My mom walked up to Selfie. "This is the first time we've met, and I—I'd just feel better if I talked to your mom and introduced myself. Since you're giving Becca a ride. Is that okay?"

"*Totally.*" Selfie nodded. "We're kind of, like, not speaking right now, cuz she won't let me pierce my belly button? But you can def call her."

"Oh." My mom didn't look reassured. "Okay."

"Nice meeting you!" Selfie handed my mom a business card as she floated out the door.

"Wait up, Selfie!" I shouted back.

"'*Selfie*'...?" my mom repeated, confused.

"Just go with it, Mom," I said, flying out of the house.

· · ● · ·

While Reinhardt drove us to school, we caught up.

"So...?" Selfie turned to me. "Spill!"

Deep breath. "Well, the guys all said you're a babe...."

She smiled and bit her lip, clearly sensing a "but" coming.

"But you sometimes come off a *little*..." I fidgeted

with my keys. "Just a tiny bit...um...'intimidating.'" I looked away.

Selfie looked wounded. "That's wack! I'm not *intimidating.*" She tapped Reinhardt on the back. "Can I have my lunch?"

"Certainly, Miss." He handed her a fancy restaurant bag.

"Selfie." I sighed. "Andy Warhol painted your mom's picture. Your household staff includes a full-time gift wrapper. You donated your old dollhouse to a museum. *Of course* these guys worry they're not exciting enough."

"But I don't *need* excitement." She frowned. "I'm happy just going out for pizza."

Weirdly, I believed her. Doing ordinary things often seemed like an adventure to her. Selfie was surprisingly down-to-earth for someone who'd been to Lady Gaga's birthday party. But how could we convince the guys at school?

"What else did they say?" Selfie sank lower in her seat.

"That you don't go out with eighth graders."

"Not true!" Selfie huffed. "Rafael was in eighth grade—"

"When you were in sixth?" I guessed.

Selfie buried her head in her hands. "Oh, Becks. I don't want to be known as a spoiled brat. What can we do?"

Truth was, I wasn't sure. Could we rebrand her, like a new kind of detergent?

The gigantic limo pulled up to the school, passing

all the kids who had taken the bus or walked.

"I'll do a reset!" Selfie sat up suddenly. "Show everyone how regular I am. Down-to-earth. Boringly normal."

Normal? I couldn't see it. I raised my eyebrow. "Yeah?"

"Yeah." Selfie lifted her chin. "I just need practice. I'm going to scream 'approachable.' Blend in with the scenery. I'll be so under the radar, I'll be just like . . ."

She paused, looking at me eagerly. "You."

Chapter 6

"*C*an I sit here?"

With four little words,
Selfie had broken the most
basic rule of middle
school: *Don't sit where you
don't belong.* Eighth-grade
fashionistas didn't mix
with sixth-grade trivia
nerds. But here she was,
standing at our cafeteria table with a lunch tray.

Rosa and Prezbo were too stunned to speak.

"Sit down," I said, patting the seat. I was startled, too.

Prezbo tucked his shirt into his pants, and even Rosa sat up straighter. People tended to do that around Selfie.

Selfie planted her purse on the table, along with her pile of "essentials": a large thermos of coffee, a bag from a fancy restaurant, an infinity scarf, a monogrammed coin purse, and vanilla cupcake body butter. (Somehow, it was never *books*.)

"What's that?" Rosa pointed to a mini suitcase.

"My makeup kit."

"You lug that around?" Rosa asked. She didn't even wear sunblock, much less makeup.

"I know, right?" Selfie made a face.

Rosa raised her eyebrows. This was going to be interesting.

"Move over," I ordered Prezbo. He didn't seem to hear me. Sitting across from the most glamorous girl in school had put him in a state of shock, so I rammed him sideways.

"So why are you sitting with us?" Rosa asked Selfie.

Prezbo and I chuckled uncomfortably.

"Just felt like changing it up." Selfie flashed her most beautiful smile. Suddenly I knew she was trying out her new personality—the one that was "ordinary" and "approachable."

"Don't let me interrupt," Selfie urged, pulling a fancy boxed lunch out of a bag. "Go on! Pretend I'm not here."

Somehow, she was hard to ignore.

None of us spoke. With her here, our favorite topics were out of the question: the lameness of the "cool" crowd, debate team gossip, the latest prom outrage. And Selfie and I couldn't discuss *our* usual obsession: finding her a date. The only sound was Prezbo draining his chocolate milk.

"What are you eating?" he asked Selfie, probably trying for a safe subject.

"Tiger shrimp with ponzu dipping sauce," said Selfie. As she opened the box, we saw pieces of food artfully arranged on a bed of tree bark. She snapped a picture with her phone.

Rosa and Prezbo looked at each other. None of *us* had photoworthy lunches.

"What did you bring?" Selfie asked politely.

"Peanut butter 'n' pickles," Rosa said, with a full mouth.

Prezbo pointed to his tray. "Cafeteria slop."

My turn. "Tuna fish."

I desperately racked my brain for a topic. We all went to the same school, right? *This shouldn't be so hard.*

"So . . . !" Selfie smiled at us all excitedly. "What's everyone doing for break?"

Silence again.

Rosa chewed a pickle. "I'm trying to get to a whole new level with my yo-yoing."

Selfie didn't know what to say to *that.*

Prezbo cleared his throat importantly. "I'll be shooting a short film, *Vampire Ice Truckers,* on my phone. Schedule's pretty tight."

I rolled my eyes. Even Prezbo—who hated every-thing the Dance Committee stood for—couldn't resist the chance to impress her. So what if he didn't like sports and wore sweaters his mother knit? He was *still* a guy.

Finally, Rosa asked Selfie, "Where are *you* going for break?"

"Oh, nowhere special." She shrugged, squeezing lime juice onto a shrimp. "The Caribbean."

"Really?" Rosa leaned forward. "What island?" Her friendly question made me grateful.

Selfie wiped her mouth with a napkin woven out of bamboo, or straw, or something. "It doesn't have a name. Our family's, like . . ." Selfie suddenly looked nervous. "The only ones who go there."

"Hold on!" Rosa pointed. "You have your *own* island?"

Selfie lowered her head. "Kinda."

Rosa and Prezbo and I just stared. Even *I* didn't know she was that rich.

Selfie continued. "But it's, you know, a trade-off. There's no pro shop or swim-up bar."

She must have sensed she was blowing it in the "ordinary" department, because she shrank back and took a hasty gulp of sparkling water.

Suddenly voices rang out behind us. "*There* you are!"

A cloud of French perfume attacked my nostrils. I spun around and saw D'Nise, Vivienne, and Chaz.

"Selfie! Girl, we didn't know *where* you were." D'Nise was out of breath. "Viv thought you were getting a facial, or—"

During a school day? Rosa's and Prezbo's eyes got even wider.

"Eyebrow wax—" Vivienne panted.

"Or you'd flown to New York to go shopping," D'Nise interrupted. They were all talking fast.

"Nope." Selfie shook her head coolly and smiled. "Just chillin' with these guys."

We all sat up a little straighter. The most popular eighth grader in school made it sound like hanging out with us was no big deal—just something she did sometimes. D'Nise looked at Prezbo, Rosa, and me with raised eyebrows.

"We just saw Clementine's post," Chaz burst out. "She says you have a superhot date for prom!"

Clementine—the prom-gossip queen?

My stomach clenched, remembering what I'd said to Clementine in her bedroom. *"Selfie's got a very cool date lined up. You'll see."*

Vivienne poked Selfie. "Well? WHO IS HE?"

D'Nise pushed aside Prezbo's lunch tray and sat on the table. People were staring. Oh, *crud.*

"Spill," D'Nise ordered.

The whole cafeteria went silent, waiting for an answer.

Rosa and Prezbo looked around. Our table had never been the center of attention before.

"Clem said that?" I choked out, stalling for time. Selfie looked too dazed to talk.

"Yeah! See?" Chaz held out his phone.

"Who? Who? Who?" A chant rocked the lunchroom. Looking at the sea of faces, I realized everyone was on their feet.

"I CAN'T TELL!" Selfie exploded. "I wish I could, but I can't. Because of, of—" She paused.

I couldn't *imagine* what was next.

"Security reasons," Selfie finished. "He's too famous."

"TOO FAMOUS?" Everyone gasped, delighted.

Oh no. Now the world's stupidest lie was even bigger.

Even Rosa and Prezbo were practically drooling. Musician? TV star? President's son? After Selfie's private island, nothing sounded too outrageous.

"HOLD ON!" Roxxi zoomed toward us, parting the crowd as if she had to perform emergency CPR. "If a celebrity's coming? That's *serious*. We're going to have to take prom up a notch."

Celebrity? A wave of nausea shot through me.

"Who? Who? Who?" The chant kept coming.

Selfie and I exchanged desperate looks.

How are we going to get out of this one?

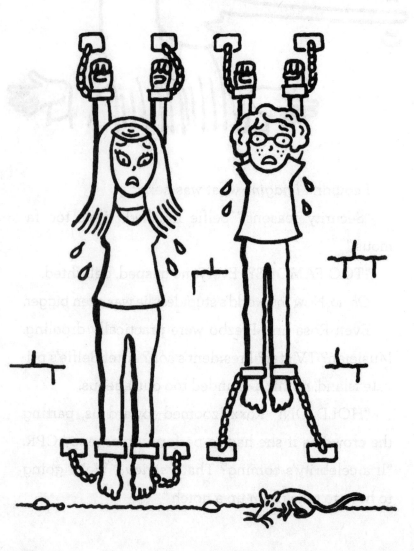

Chapter 7

From then on, everywhere Selfie went, people tried to guess her prom date.

"Is he on TV?"

"The junior tennis star with the ponytail?"

"Is he in the royal family?"

Selfie just smiled and kept walking. I hadn't been able to talk to her since she'd dropped the bombshell about her date being "famous," making my job even harder. Now school had finally ended, but we had to meet someone about Dance Committee business.

The timing sucked.

"Who are we meeting with?" I asked, irritated.

"A seventh grader who has some ideas for prom. We just have to hear him out."

We arrived at the Multi-Purpose Room. Selfie sank into a plastic seat and stretched her legs, like it was a beach chair at Club Med. She kicked off her three-inch heels.

"I'm *exhausted*," she moaned, pulling out a bottle of Italian sparkling water.

I was worried sick. Since lunch, my chances of finding her a date had gone from Very Difficult to No Freakin' Way.

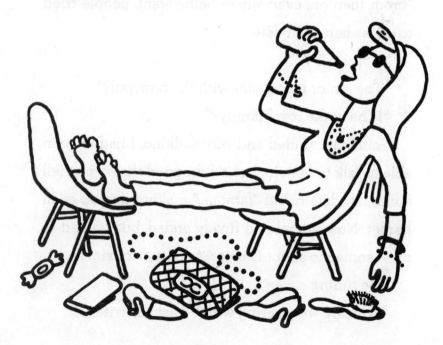

"Listen, Selfie." I took a deep breath. "I know it was tough today. But saying your date was 'famous' creates, you know, *expectations*."

Selfie sat up.

"Well, you messed up, too!" She took off her sunglasses. "Telling the school's biggest gossip I had a hot date . . . !"

"I know." Guilt soured my stomach. "But you made it a lot worse. Who am I supposed to get? First he just had to be handsome, cool, and amazing. Now he has to be *famous*, too?"

Selfie looked at the floor and bit her lip.

"Look, I know you want an amazing date," I said gently. "But there's nothing wrong with going to prom alone. Or with your friends! The point is to have fun, not to totally *stress out*."

Selfie was silent.

Knock-knock. Selfie jumped up to open the door. With a drink in her hand, she looked like she was welcoming guests to a dinner party.

"Hi, Dinesh!" Selfie looked back at me and winked.

As in . . . *Dinesh O'Reilly*?

That's who we were meeting with? *CRUUUUUUDDDDD!*

My hands immediately flew to my hair. I fluffed it up, then smoothed out my jeans. Why had I worn this stupid rainbow tee? I looked like I was nine.

"I'm Dinesh," he said.

I tried to meet Selfie's eyes. She'd tricked us into meeting! I wasn't ready for face-to-face contact. I felt like I was going to throw up.

"Salutations," said someone else, in a high, nasal voice.

A guy walked out from behind Dinesh wearing a lightning-bolt baseball cap. It was Felix Needleman, the unibrowed sixth-grade supernerd. As usual, he carried a backpack the size of a microwave.

He and Dinesh were a strange pair. As if reading my mind, Dinesh explained, "We're in robotics together. He's just tagging along."

Still playing party hostess, Selfie motioned for us to sit down.

Felix dived for the chair next to Selfie. "Breath strip?" he offered. She shook her head.

Selfie put on sunglasses and started applying a fragrant goop to her arms. It looked like she was sunbathing.

Felix was openly staring.

Dinesh got to the point. "So! Selfie says you guys are interested in having a green prom."

Oh, really? I thought, almost laughing. *You mean Selfie, that famous environmental activist?*

Selfie shot me a look like, *I had to get him here somehow.*

Turning to Dinesh, she said, "I'm very interested, but honestly? I'm not great with details . . ."

No kidding. She barely wrote down homework assignments, never wore a watch, and her only pen sprouted a pink feather.

" . . . so you should really talk to Becca," she continued.

"YES!" I tried to sound calm.

"Cool," he said. "I've got tons of ideas."

He went on about compostable plates and carpooling—but I barely heard it. I couldn't look him in the eye, so instead I focused on his backpack buttons.

Then the door banged open, and Roxxi stormed in. "Selfie, we need more fairy lights for the Golden Memories Arch, so—"

She stopped in midsentence. We weren't an easy group to sort out: handsome Dinesh, nerdy Felix drooling at Selfie, and the Queen Bee stretched out like she was poolside in Acapulco.

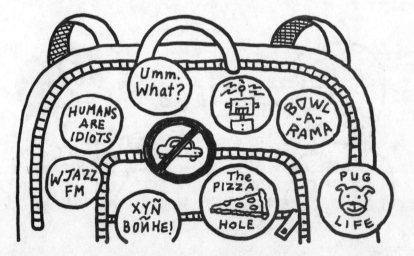

"Hi, Roxxi." Selfie waved. "This is Dinesh, and, uh—"

"Needleman. Felix Needleman," he said, making it sound like "Bond. James Bond." He tipped his lightning bolt hat.

"Selfie wants to make prom more eco-friendly," I dared. "So Dinesh is giving us ideas."

Roxxi looked alarmed. "What does *that* mean?"

Dinesh swallowed. "Well, cutting waste, to start—"

Roxxi raised her eyebrows. "We're bare-bones as it is. What could we cut? The snow globes for the gift bags? The nonalcoholic champagne tower?"

"Uh—"

"The chocolate infinity fountain? The floating sushi bar?"

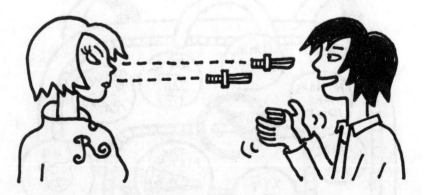

Dinesh looked at me helplessly. The door banged open again.

"Yo, Selfie?" It was Ajax, the school's biggest bully, sticking his head through the door. "Is it Junior Mintt?"

"What?" Selfie asked.

"Your prom date. Is it Junior Mintt?" Ajax struck a gangster pose, imitating the twelve-year-old rapper.

Felix's eyes widened.

"No." Selfie's voice was weary.

"Someone in Gummy Rat? Little Bigger?" Behind him, Ajax's friends, B.B. and Scab, were guessing, too.

"CAN'T YOU SEE WE'RE IN A MEETING?" Roxxi scolded. "Morons."

Ajax and his friends left. Roxxi turned back to Dinesh. "Sorry! What were you saying about . . ." She smiled politely. "Ruining prom?"

Dinesh took a deep breath. "A green prom's more doable than you think. Maybe it seems like a lot to ask to go paperless, or recycle. But these sacrifices really add up to help the planet. I'm just trying to get people involved."

Not only was he cute—he wanted to make the world better.

"Cool," said Selfie. Roxxi rolled her eyes.

"Why don't you make a list of ideas?" I asked Dinesh shyly. "We can at least—I don't know—*think* about them." He gave me a truly amazing smile.

But Roxxi glared at me. "Who asked *you*? You're just a sixth grader! You don't have the power to ..."

She went on for a while, and Selfie defended me, but I wasn't really listening. I didn't care about Roxxi, or gondolas, or snow globes.

I was in love.

THUMP
THUMP
THUMP

After the meeting ended, I raced over to Burger Freak to hang with Rosa and Prezbo. Luckily, they were still there. Prezbo was attacking his usual pre-dinner hamburger, while Rosa slurped an Atomic Shake. I ordered onion rings.

Rosa slid a napkin in front of me.

"We just came up with this." Rosa's eyes had a naughty gleam. "Cool, huh?"

"Prom shpelled backward." Prezbo's mouth was full. "Get it?"

Anti-prom?

Rosa went on. "We were just sitting around, doing crossword puzzles, when *they* sat down. . . ." She tipped her head toward the girls at the next booth. I looked over to see Dance Committee members D'Nise, Ashleigh, and Vivienne sharing gossip and a hot fudge sundae.

"We overheard all this insane stuff . . ." Rosa whispered. "The Dance Committee's raising the ticket price to sixty dollars! That's wack!"

"Yikes." I gulped. *Glad Selfie's getting me a free ticket.* "That's a lot, but I know costs have really added up. You'd be surprised how much—"

"Are you defending it?" Rosa's voice rose.

"No! No." *Awkward.* "I was just explaining—"

Voices floated over from the Cool Girls' booth.

"... know of a good brow specialist?" ... "My hair-and-makeup team ..."

Rosa made gagging noises. "So we wondered: What if there was a dance for *us*?"

"Where you could play foosball, and Scrabble," said Prezbo, wiping his mouth. "Eat Twizzlers. Sit on beanbag chairs."

"Wear what we're wearing now." Rosa tugged her T-shirt.

Inside, I thought, *Really? That's your special, once-a-year event?*

"So we thought," Rosa said, "why not have an anti-prom? On the same night as the dance, but everything's the opposite. They have sushi—"

"We eat Oreos." Prezbo munched.

"They have long dresses—"

"We wear sweats," he finished.

No! No! No!

I wanted to go to prom—*the real one*. I wanted to walk through clouds of mist from a fog machine and gawk at the super-glam gowns. I wanted to sign the fancy guest book and refresh my lip balm in the girls' bathroom. And now I had something new to dream about.

Rosa's cheeks flushed. "So I said—"

"Why not have our own!" Prezbo interrupted.

"Do stuff that's *fun*." Rosa started a drum solo on the table. "Video games, trivia contests, graffiti-writing . . ."

"My playlist of old TV theme songs," Prezbo added.

"Decorate with lava lamps, old vinyl album covers. Skateboard art!"

Skateboard art? In spite of myself, I felt a stirring of interest. What other oddball things would they come up with?

"Forget the stupid Dude 'n' Diva Awards." Prezbo almost spit the words out. "We'd give prizes for things that matter: Best Palindrome. Weirdest Sharpie Tattoo. Highest Monopoly Score."

I burst into a laugh. It sounded fun, but . . .

"Guys! Guys!" I made a time-out sign. "Neither of you has ever showed the slightest interest in *going* to a party, much less throwing one."

Rosa shrugged. Prezbo licked his fingers.

"Where would you hold it?" I joked. "The school *basement*?"

Uncomfortable silence.

"The bugs are mostly in the boiler room," Rosa pointed out.

Oh boy.

"How about the smell?" I asked.

"What do you think air freshener's for?" Rosa looked annoyed.

"Listen, guys—" *Don't hate me, but . . .* "This would be a TON of work. And you're not exactly 'party organizers.'"

Rosa looked hurt. "If I can put together a paintball war with players at three different skill levels, I *think* I can handle some dopey party."

"And *I* set up that comic book swap," Prezbo reminded me.

"Besides . . ." Rosa smiled. "We have *you*."

"ME?"

"You're doing all this stuff for *Selfie* . . ." Prezbo's eyes lingered on me. "But we've known you a lot longer."

Oh no. No, no, no.

"I-I can't," I stammered. "I'm already behind on helping Selfie. I don't have time to plan Morp! And if it's the *same night*? I don't even know if I can *go*."

"WHAT?" Rosa and Prezbo cried.

"I'm kind of committed to prom already."

Rosa and Prezbo looked flattened. My head was throbbing. Suddenly, we were on different sides of the Grand Canyon.

Boy, was it lonely.

How did I get here? I wasn't sure. It's not like I wanted to abandon my friends. But for one night— *one night!*—I wanted to drink pink juice from a punch bowl and wear a jeweled barrette in my hair. Was that so terrible?

"Actually, I *want* to go," I admitted. "To prom, I mean."

The Grand Canyon got even wider. Prezbo scowled and pushed his basket away. Rosa's table drumming got more furious. We had never disagreed like this before.

I couldn't take it.

"*Okay.*" I sighed. "I'll help out. I'll come to meetings, draw the poster, wear the T-shirt. I just can't be in charge. And if it's really just downstairs from prom, I'll try to go to both." Somehow, I'd make it work.

Rosa was still stewing but seemed to realize this was my best offer. "I don't know when you got to be *Ms. Prom*, but okay, yeah, whatever."

Prezbo continued his silent brooding. Finally, he grunted, "Are you going to eat that onion ring?" I took it as a peace offering.

I'd avoided disaster, but it still felt like hanging off a cliff by my fingernails. Admitting I wanted something different from them felt dangerous. We needed one another. We'd sort of worked it out for now, but...

How long can you hang from a cliff?

Chapter 9

I walked to the bulletin board outside the school office. The second I sank the thumbtack in, I heard Roxxi's voice.

"OMG," she gasped. "*You're* behind this?"

I stepped back, as if to distance myself from the poster I'd drawn. Too late.

Roxxi, D'Nise, and Vivienne leaned in to read it, making little sounds of disgust.

"You come to our meetings . . . then work for the *enemy*?" Roxxi's voice shook with outrage.

"I'm not *behind* anything," I said. "I'm just helping out my friends."

They looked unmoved.

"Some people just aren't prom-goers," I explained. "They can't afford it. Hate crepe paper. Whatever. This party's for *them*."

Roxxi and D'Nise sniffed, trying to imagine such a person.

"You don't get it, do you?" Vivienne sighed. "*We need to sell, like, every ticket.* You know how much we're spending! If we don't make that money back . . ."

"It's on *you*." D'Nise poked my shoulder.

When I'd volunteered to help Morp, I hadn't thought about how the Dance Committee would react.

Too bad this had come up now, just when they were starting to tolerate me. Sometimes they even nodded hello or asked my opinion.

They liked how I could unjam the copy machine, get Selfie to a 7:30 a.m. meeting, and spell *bouton-niere*. I liked how they could transform a basketball hoop into a Paris streetlamp. They were like artists, but instead of pencils or paint, they used glitter, silk, and fairy lights. And they did work *very* hard.

Now we'd go back to silent stares and eye rolls.

"Let's get out of here," Roxxi said glumly.

"Wait!" I tugged D'Nise's sleeve. "What are you worried about? How can Oreos in a basement com-pete with *prom*—the most glamorous night at school?"

They broke into relieved smiles. *Of course* Morp couldn't compete with prom. We all relaxed a bit, chuckling at how they'd gotten carried away. Then Roxxi cleared her throat, as if to remind them they were still mad at me. I watched as they marched off down the hall.

· · ● · ·

The Morp planning meeting was packed.

"Where are we going to put everyone?" Rosa whispered. Who would have guessed the power of the word *anti-prom*? Every nerd, misfit, and rebel at school had come out of the woodwork to attend.

Prezbo and Rosa scrambled around, trying to find chairs. Nothing we'd ever done before had attracted this much interest.

"Sit on the pipes," Rosa urged people. "Steam only comes out, like, once an hour."

"Spider alert!" A goth girl pointed to the floor.

Prezbo walked to the front of the room, clearing his throat. The audience looked at him suspiciously.

"Wow." Prezbo's eyes widened. He wasn't used to speaking to a crowd. "I can't believe all the people here. We're—"

Someone's phone made a digitized *Pow! Pow!* sound.

"—anxious for your ideas about Morp," Prezbo went on. "I don't know what you think about prom, but—"

"BOOOOOOOOO!"

Ajax cupped his hands. "PROM SUCKS!"

People made their feelings known.

"Heh-heh." Prezbo wiped his brow. "Okay, okay. This isn't—it's not about trashing prom. It's about having our *own* party. Something for us."

"Who's '*us*'?" Slash Dobbins asked sharply. He was a graffiti artist whose gray hoodie fit like a second skin. It was a good question, because except for hating prom, it was unclear whether this group had anything—at all—in common.

Prezbo looked around the room. "You know, the ones who aren't playing travel tennis, or eating sliders at the country club. People who aren't 'cool.'" He made quotation marks in the air.

"Losers, you mean." A girl with cat glasses smiled.

Prezbo shook his head, taking her seriously. "No, I don't think so. It's being . . . weird, in a good way, or wanting something . . . more."

"*More?*" someone repeated.

"Something more . . . *you*," Prezbo tried to explain. "Not going along with whatever the crowd says, like

'Rap's the only cool music' or 'That's a girl movie.'"

"Huh?" Slash looked confused.

Listening to Prezbo made my heart twist. A noisy meeting probably wasn't the best place to explain his life philosophy. But his wanting to stick up for us "different" types really got to me.

"What he means is . . ." Rosa jumped in. "Why do we let *them* tell us to get dates and spend money we don't have? We need our own party! WHO'S WITH US?"

She looked around for support, but people were looking at the ceiling, shuffling their feet, or chewing their nails. They all hated prom, but they weren't sure about Morp. What was it going to *be*, exactly?

Someone's hand shot up. "What are you doing for music? My band could use the gig."

That set off a loud argument. "I have a band, too!" "Ours is better!" "No band—DEEJAY!"

"Uhhh—" Rosa looked at Prezbo helplessly. "We haven't really . . ."

More people shouted ques-
tions.

"Are pets allowed?"

"Will there be gluten-free
desserts?"

"Can you wear flip-flops?"

Rosa and Prezbo looked
overwhelmed. "One at a time!"
Rosa wiped her forehead with a
bandanna. "Maybe we should
go around and say what we
want from Morp."

Maya Borgatta raised her hand. I stared at her
elaborately pierced ear.

"I think Morp is a chance to have an honest dialogue about gender, race, and stereotyping," she said.
"With vegetarian appetizers."

"Uh-huh. Okay." Rosa and I exchanged worried
looks. That sounded Important, but not super-fun.
"Anyone else?"

Ajax stepped out of the shadows. "I say we sneak into
prom and mess stuff *up*." He smiled. "All we need is chili
powder, some highway flares, and a loose ferret."

"Do we have to have it here?" asked a girl with tiny stuffed animals attached to her pigtails. "It smells like *puke*."

"No, the basement's cool," Lilith Blumberg assured her. "Makes it more like a rave. We could have, like, all-black decorations. And a hand stamp. You *have* to have a hand stamp."

People were finally getting into it. Even die-hard cranks and loners were chiming in with demands like "Harry Potter trivia!" or "Seven-foot subs!"

"SKATE JAM!" rasped Finn Petrokis, a skate punk who spoke in a lazy voice. He lifted a bandaged arm to pump his fist.

"Skate. JAM. Skate. JAM. Skate—" chanted the other skaters.

"Spoken-word poetry and a selection of herbal teas!" Frieda Wong-Suarez shouted.

There was a noise in the hall—a clatter of heels and bags rustling together.

All eyes turned toward the door.

Holy crud.

Selfie's arrival was met with gasps. "O. M. G." "What the . . . ?" "No freakin' *way*." And then, dead silence. People watched in disbelief as she floated through the basement, carrying shopping bags and throwing back her blond hair, hurrying toward me.

"Becca—do you have my keys? Cuz I can't find—"

"Sit down," Prezbo whispered.

"Oh. Thanks," Selfie said airily, as she settled on a drum of barf-absorbent sawdust. Her shopping bags hit the floor with a thud. When she sat down, her three-inch heeled gold sandals stood out from the sea of army boots and beat-up sneakers.

Everyone was still in shock.

"Go ahead!" Selfie made a shooing gesture to Prezbo. "Have your meeting and whatevs! I'll talk to Becca later—"

Her phone rang. "Oh, hi," she whispered, as the whole room strained to hear. "I'm in a meeting. No, *not* with a stylist."

Prezbo cleared his throat, but everyone was listening to Selfie. Finally, I had to go up to her and whisper, "Shhhh!" I could feel everyone stare.

"You *know* her?" someone asked.

Maya smirked. "Becca's on the Dance Committee."

She pointed at me like she was ID'ing a criminal.

A ripple went through the crowd. I shot a look at Selfie, but she was buried in her phone. Everyone's eyes drilled into me.

"Whose side are you on?" Finn's chin jutted out.

"Uh . . ." *Crud.* I didn't like being in the spotlight. My palms were sweaty. My eyes moved to Rosa and Prezbo, begging for help. But strangely, they were waiting for an answer, too.

"I'm not taking sides," I said nervously.

"You're either with us or against us," a guy in surgical scrubs sniffed.

The room seemed like a pot about to boil over. *This is what happens when half the school feels permanently left out.* Twenty minutes ago, this cranky group had been impossible to organize. Now they'd united against a common enemy.

Me.

Selfie's phone rang again, but this time, she ducked outside to take the call.

Shouts and arguing broke out in the basement. For a second, I thought they were going to pick up the janitor's mops and throw them at me. I was scared.

"Leave her alone!"

It was Dinesh. He came up and put his arm around me.

When had he gotten here?

"She's just trying to help," he explained. "Those prom guys aren't the enemy. They just want a different party."

My insides turned liquid. He was defending me! Not only was he cute, and a do-gooder, he had *guts*.

I smiled at him gratefully. He tipped an imaginary hat.

"Yeah, yeah." Prezbo seemed eager to shoo Dinesh away, so we slipped off to the side. "Okay, guys, what have we decided?"

"Battle of the bands!" shouted someone.

"Honest political dialogue," said Mia.

"PRANK THOSE SNOBS!" Ajax, Scab, and B.B. yelled.

"We could just play games on our phones," suggested Xander Katlin.

"Vir-tu-al par-ty," Felix Needleman said in a robot voice.

"Stop. STOP. *STOP!*" Prezbo shouted to the whole group.

People looked at him, startled.

"Is there anything, and I mean *anything* . . ." He gasped for breath. " . . . we CAN agree on?"

People kicked the floor, snapped their gum, and jiggled loose coins.

No one had an answer.

Chapter 10

"SICK GRAB!"

"TEAR IT UP!"

"YOU GOT THIS!"

Selfie and I were at Grindapalooza, a skateboard festival on the other side of the city. All around us, guys in knitted caps and rude T-shirts were screaming. Everyone was watching thirteen-year-old whiz kid Montana Smith.

We held our breath as Montana zoomed up the ramp and soared into the air. He spun around one and a half times and landed smoothly. The crowd roared, and he broke into a goofy smile. *Look, I got away with it again*, his eyes said. His surprise at himself was charming.

"He's cute," I said.

"Cute?" Selfie's eyes followed him down the ramp. "He's smokin' *hot*."

Good, I thought with relief.

"YEAHHHH!" The crowd cheered more.

Montana didn't know we were checking him out as a possible prom date. I'd learned about him in a magazine left behind at the Morp meeting.

When I read he lived in a nearby suburb, my heart jumped. He was famous, local, and had a charity that recycled skateboards for homeless kids! He was *perfect*.

I had a pitch prepared about why he should come to our prom, how his visit would inspire students, blah, blah, blah. Of course, Selfie was the main attraction—when I explained she'd be his date, he'd be too dazzled to say no.

I followed Selfie to the long line leading to the autograph table, past a sea of taped knees and bandaged elbows. No one else looked like they'd arrived by limo. As we moved along, everyone stared at the beautiful blonde.

"Hey." A kid behind us smiled at Selfie, showing missing teeth. "You rip?" She looked at him blankly, so he tried again. "You skate?"

"No," Selfie said coolly.

"Too bad." He leered at her.

More guys circled around her. "Going to the X Games?" "Want some Skittles?" "Where *you* from?"

"Excuse me." Selfie turned her back and huddled with me, ending the conversation. She pointed to Montana, who was busily signing away. "I hope he has a tux," she whispered. "He's *adorbs*."

Inching closer to the table, I realized we weren't the only ones who thought so.

Selfie smiled. "They have *no idea* what they're up against." Her confidence gave me a little thrill.

At last we got to the front of the line. A guy in a Hawaiian shirt and gray man-bun said, "We've got a long line, so make it quick."

"Hey." Montana nodded at us. Up close, we could see a hook-shaped scar near his eyebrow and his bumpy, blistered hands. Somehow, they just made him more appealing. He took in Selfie's high-fashion outfit. "You a skate rat?"

"No, but—" Selfie was apologetic. "We're big fans. Some of those flips were, like, *insane*."

"Thanks." His goofy smile came back.

I jumped in. "Listen, our school is having a prom in a couple weeks, and we were wondering..."

At the word *prom*, his eyes went dead. "No thanks."

Selfie gasped. I blinked rapidly.

"I hate school dances." He made a face.

Crud. "Are you sure?" I begged. "Because your being there would be, like, so inspiring—"

He cut me off. "Sorry. Can't."

Just then a girl came up behind him and slapped Montana's back. "Thanks again, dude. See you at the rescue dogs benefit."

So he liked good causes. I wondered if we could invent one. Preteens with Allergies? Scrapbookers Without Borders? Was there any way to convince him our prom wasn't a regular prom?

"You know . . ." I babbled, trying to keep him interested. "Our school's also having an anti-prom, called Morp."

Selfie gave me a sideways look.

"What's Morp?" he asked suspiciously.

"It's . . ." *Good question.* "The opposite of prom. With, uh, vegan desserts and skateboard art."

He lifted an eyebrow. "Skateboard art?"

"Maybe," I said.

"Hurry up!" someone behind us shouted.

I handed him a Morp flyer. "There's lots more! What time are you done? We'll wait for you over—"

Man-Bun interrupted. "I'm Arlo, his manager. You want to hire him for something? Mall opening? Sweet sixteen? Party boat?"

"No, we—"

"Then move along." He shooed us away.

I glanced back at Montana, but he was already signing other autographs.

In the car, Selfie and I didn't look at each other. We'd struck out again.

I was in a dressing room at the mall, helping Selfie try on a sequined hoodie. "It's for the third stage of prom," she explained. "*After* the after-party."

"Right." I was only pretending to pay attention. I was thinking about the List: all the possibilities for Selfie's celebrity prom date.

Trouble was, the List kept getting shorter.

As each day passed, the odds were worse and worse. How long could we keep pretending this was all going to work out?

"You've got to see this pic." Selfie tossed me her phone. "This guy I sort of know just sent it. He's the one with the scarf."

I quickly shut my notebook.

He was handsome, whoever he was. It looked like a professional photo. I could almost feel the cold air and taste the hot chocolate. He wore a white sweater under his scarf, and a flashy watch.

I couldn't believe she knew guys like that. "Who is he?"

"His name is Jean-Luc. We went to camp

Reality show guy — not interested

13 yr. old chef (left message 5x)

Informercial Kid (sent 7 texts)

Australian pop star? (too busy)

e-sports champ — No!

guy from Tween Wolf (agent hung up) :(

Deejay Cody G.

Disney Show goy (left 10 9 messages)

YouTube fashion blogger?? Nope.

together." Everyone knew about Selfie's famous, fancy summer camp in Switzerland.

"How old is he?"

"Fourteen." She started chattering on about his big-deal family. Apparently, they owned a castle, a bunch of racehorses, and, possibly, a mountain range.

I yawned. Unless he lived within driving distance and owned a tux, I wasn't interested. Selfie tried on a ripped T-shirt.

A knock on the dressing room door. "How are you doing? Can I get you something?"

A date for prom, I thought glumly.

Selfie opened the door, handing back some

rejected clothes. "Do you have the torn T-shirt in a size five?"

"On it!" chirped the salesgirl. "And try this." She handed Selfie a blouse that looked like a cheerleader's pom-pom.

"I wish you could find me someone like Jean-Luc." Selfie sighed, pulling the shirt over her head.

Was she *serious?* I didn't know gorgeous, European rich guys.

"Selfie! I—"

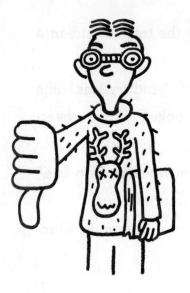

"You know, he doesn't have to be . . . *famous*, exactly." She gave a little smile. "We could lower our standards a little."

I sighed. What she didn't realize was . . .

I already had.

That morning, I'd talked to Todd Flegenheim, a brilliant but weird eighth-grade science fair winner.

Even *he* turned her down. But of course, I couldn't tell *her* that.

Now, as she stood there in a feathered top, looking like Big Bird, I felt my insides melt. Her eyes were so hopeful! The thought of disappointing her made my stomach turn.

"Okay." I swallowed. "We'll widen the search."

When we got back to the limo, Reinhardt said, "A young man dropped this off." He held up a piece of notebook paper, folded in half.

A tingle ran up the back of my neck. Selfie finally, *finally* had a prom date! Who could it be? One of the jocks? The YouTube star? Had Montana Smith changed his mind?

We scrambled into the back seat. Selfie unfolded the note. I watched her eyes widen. "Tell me!" I begged. Finally, she slid the paper onto my lap.

"It's for you," she said.

Chapter 11

The next day at school, my hand kept dipping into my jeans pocket. That's where I kept the note.

I couldn't believe it. Dinesh had offered me a ride. *Me!* Clearly, he was new at school and didn't know

how things worked. Handsome, popular seventh graders didn't reach out to short, bookish sixth graders. Somehow, he hadn't gotten the memo.

It was mind-blowing—but I couldn't be completely happy. I felt too guilty over Selfie not having a date. When we discovered the note was for me, Selfie handled it gracefully, squealing with excitement. But when she turned away, her eyes looked suspiciously shiny.

It wasn't until school let out that I spotted Dinesh's wild black hair in the crowded hall. I ran up and tapped his shoulder.

"I got your note!" I shouted above the noise.

He broke into a smile. "Good! Yes!"

He moved closer so we didn't have to shout. My pulse jumped.

"Thanks, I—" *Be cool.* "A ride would be good."

"Happy to help." He gave a jokey formal bow. "We're picking up other people, too."

"Oh!" I tried to smile. "Cool."

My disappointment must have shown, because he shifted his backpack and cleared his throat. "It's not, like, a date, or anything, but . . ." He looked at the floor. "I hear you like to dance, right?"

"Sure." *YEEEEESSSSS!*

"Well, when we get there, you and I should—"

"Hey, Dinesh!" Sofia Mellins ran up, practically tackling him. "We need to talk about the endangered species fund-raiser."

CRUD! What awful timing. Of course a guy like that would have other girls buzzing around.

He turned back to me. "Sorry, I have to deal with this. We'll settle details later."

"Okay." I waved good-bye. But my heart was pumping wildly.

I floated down the hall in a daze. What would he wear? A classic suit and tie? A tux and red high-tops? Would the driver honk the horn and wait, or would Dinesh come in and meet my parents? Would he dance like a guy in a hip-hop video or twirl me around the old-fashioned way?

In the middle of my daydream, I passed a Morp poster. *Crud!* I'd totally forgotten I was supposed to help Rosa and Prezbo. I turned around and ran.

When I got to the Multi-Purpose Room, I found them huddled over Prezbo's laptop. They barely grunted hello as I grabbed a chair.

"Listen to this." Prezbo tapped a key.

I cupped my ear. "Is something playing?"

All I could hear was a faint tinkling, like ice cubes in a glass. Then a distant chime and the sound of shifting sand. "Too sensitive," complained Prezbo.

"So much for Gregopolis." Rosa frowned. "Cross 'em off."

"We're choosing a band for Morp," explained Prezbo. There was a pile of homemade CDs and flyers.

"Looks like lots of people are interested." My voice was upbeat. "That's good, right?"

Prezbo shrugged. "They all suck."

Rosa turned to me. "Where were you? We've been here a half an hour."

"Sorry."

Next up was a music video starring Ajax. He was rapping from a jail cell, which looked suspiciously like the school batting cage. Then he and his gang were leaning on a fancy car.

"We're three of a kind, and we'll rock your mind—"

"The rudest dudes that ya ever will find—"

We watched more clips. Seventh grader TaNisha sang a fiery girl-power anthem. Three nerds called Meh played spooky high-tech music. The Candy Rappers had matching midriff tops but terrible voices.

Prezbo threw his pen down. "Forget having a band. Let's just make a playlist and use portable speakers. Becks, can you come early to help set up?"

I swallowed.

Now was the time to tell them about riding with Dinesh. So why had I suddenly forgotten how to talk?

"I—uh—uh—"

Sweat dampened my neck. Prezbo was scrolling down his laptop. Rosa was tapping her phone screen. Finally, they looked up.

The three of us had never admitted to having crushes—those were for kids who were older, cooler, and possibly less smart. How far could we branch out in new directions and still remain best friends?

"Actually, I can't help set up," I confessed. "I'm getting a ride to prom."

"So?" Rosa shrugged. "Have your mom drop you early."

"My mom's not—" My heart was pounding. "I'm getting a ride from Dinesh O'Reilly. That new guy."

They stopped dead.

"WHAT?" Rosa turned to me, outraged. "What is this? Some kind of . . . *date*?"

"No." I snorted, looking at the floor.

Prezbo suddenly got very busy organizing files on his computer. His face looked a shade whiter.

"Dinesh O'Reilly," Rosa repeated, baffled.

"He's just being nice," I said quickly.

Of course, I'd left out crucial information, like (1) I had a huge crush on Dinesh, and that (2) Selfie had introduced us.

I felt like a rat.

"I don't believe it," Rosa muttered.

Prezbo closed the laptop and spun around. "I don't care about the *date*," he sniffed. "It's the principle of it."

"But—"

"We're supposed to be a team." His sentences came in angry bursts. "It's bad enough you're blowing us off that night, but now you can't even help *set up*?"

My heart sank. "Prezbo, I've done tons of stuff for Morp! I said I'd juggle both events, and I'm trying—"

He started packing up his laptop with barely controlled fury.

"*Don't bother,*" he said grimly.

Rosa turned to him. "Wait—*what*?"

"*DON'T* come to our meetings. *DON'T* sit with us at lunch." Prezbo's voice got louder. "*DON'T do ANY of it.*"

Rosa yanked him aside. "Prez—what are you *doing*? We need her!"

I picked up my backpack. My legs dragged me across the room. I opened the door.

"Ignore him, Becca," Rosa whispered. "He's taking this too far."

I roamed the hall like a zombie. What just happened? Was it possible . . . Prezbo was *jealous*? We'd never been "that way" with each other. Or did he just not want things to change?

"Hey!" someone down the hall was yelling. "Where's Selfie?"

Oh, *crud*. Roxxi, D'Nise, and Chaz were coming right toward me. I tried to veer away. "Not so fast," said Roxxi, blocking my path.

"Where's Selfie?" she demanded.

The truth was, Selfie was hiding out so she wouldn't have to answer questions about her Mystery Date. Right now she was at the library, because it was the last place anyone would look for her.

"She hasn't posted for hours." D'Nise was puzzled. "It's not normal."

"I texted her about a shoe sale," Chaz added. *"No answer."*

"Yesterday, she mixed gold and silver jewelry," Vivienne confided.

Everyone gasped.

"Becca, have you ever met this top secret prom date? Because *I* think ..." Roxxi pressed closer to me. *"He doesn't exist."*

"What?" I tried to sound outraged. "That's— that's—"

100 percent true.

"I've got to go," I said, slipping past them. This time, I wouldn't take the bait.

"Can you give Selfie a message?"

I stopped. What now?

"It's about the Dude 'n' Diva Awards." Roxxi smiled. She was enjoying this. "You have to register in advance. With the name of your prom date . . . and the deadline's *tomorrow*."

"*WHAT?*" Now my outrage was real. "Since when?"

"Since yesterday. Just wanted her to know," she said sweetly. She started to walk away and then turned back. "By the way, how's Morp? I heard every ticket comes with a can of RAID!"

Her friends' laughter drifted down the hall.

I leaned against a locker to catch my breath. I suddenly realized I had to tell Selfie the truth: She was going to prom alone.

CRUD! I hated to make her unhappy. She could be ridiculous, but she always stood up for people she cared about. I remembered how she'd sat next to me in Dance Committee, as if being friendly with a nerdy sixth grader was a normal thing to do. The time we'd laughed together over the principal's underwear. And how she'd been so sweet about Dinesh. She was a really, really good person.

And now . . .

I had to break her heart.

Chapter 12

The iron gates opened, and a security guard waved me inside. How many times had I passed by, wondering if I'd ever see the bowling alley in the basement or the ballroom with the lighted dance floor?

I'd always wanted to go to Selfie's house, but so far, we'd been mostly "school friends." How weird to be invited now, when I had such awful news to dump on her.

"Becca!" Selfie ran down the driveway and threw her arms around me. "I'm so glad you're here!"

I couldn't hold it in for another second.

"I'm so sorry," I burst out. "I couldn't find you a date! I feel *awful*. I tried everything, but it just wasn't—"

Selfie stopped me.

"It's okay," she said sweetly. "I already have one."

My jaw dropped.

"You *have* a date?" I almost fell over. "With who?"

Selfie led me inside, up a grand curving staircase. Above it was the kind of fancy painted dome you see in state capitols. She took me to her room and leaped onto a giant bed. She pushed aside a mountain of pillows and motioned for me to sit.

"Him!" Selfie held up her phone.

It was Jean-Luc, the ski-chalet guy from Swiss summer camp.

"Doesn't he live in France?" I was confused.

"Yes, but he's coming to America for a soccer game—*same week as prom!*" A smile spread across her face. "It just worked out."

"Wow." I was still trying to absorb it. *SELFIE HAD A DATE!*

Our worst-case scenarios would never happen. She didn't have to leave town or hire someone.

From what I remembered, the guy totally fit the bill. He wasn't famous, but he was a major catch: foreign, handsome, and Insta-worthy. *YEEESSSS!* I did a

mental fist pump. This was amazing. Now I could go back to worrying about my own problems.

Dizzy with relief, I started to look around. *Holy crud.* Selfie's bedroom was so big, it had its own living room. The place was a teen girl's fantasy, with a see-through chair hanging from the ceiling, two-foot-high SELFIE neon sign, and real polar bear rug (if polar bears were hot pink).

A spiral staircase led to the second level, where I saw a jukebox, a gumball machine, and an earring stand the size of a Christmas tree.

"Is that a real salon chair?" I jumped up and walked to a hot-pink leather chair with an adjustable hair dryer. It faced a movie-star mirror ringed by lights.

"Oh—" Selfie waved her hand. "I just use it for touch-ups."

It was also interesting to see what the room *didn't* have: books, or a comfortable place to do homework. The glass desk was sleek, stylish, and had clearly never been used. It held two items: an electric-blue feather quill pen and a bowl filled with silver balls.

Then I hit the mother lode.

I stared at Selfie's dressing table. Oh, how I wanted one! A place to try different hairstyles, dance in the mirror, write on the glass in lipstick ...

Selfie sat down at the vanity, picked up a hairbrush, and started brushing with rapid strokes. "What ever happened with Dinesh?"

I tore myself away from her perfume bottles and perched on the see-through plastic chair. "Dinesh is giving me a ride to prom." Just saying his name made my skin tingle. "I don't know details yet."

"A ride, huh? Nice." Then Selfie tilted her head. "What about Prezbo?"

"What about him?" I asked, annoyed.

Selfie shrugged. "He likes you."

WHAT?

"Who *says*?" I felt shocked, flattered, and angry all at the same time.

Selfie put down her brush.

"Hmm, let's see." Selfie counted on her fingers. "He texts you at midnight to play GamePigeon. He makes fun of your rain boots. When he says something funny, he looks sideways to see if you laughed." She sighed. "It's *obvi.*"

Selfie didn't get it. She was so used to guys flirting with her, she didn't realize girls and guys could just be friends.

"I've seen the guy in *Pokémon pajamas*," I pointed out. "We're just friends."

Used to be, anyway.

Selfie raised an eyebrow. "Okay. Whatevs. Hey, I want to show you something."

She pulled back a pair of glass doorknobs, and there it was—her famous closet! Like her bedroom, it had two floors, plus a minifridge, chandelier, and TV.

Selfie plucked out a dress from a department store–sized rack. "So . . . what do you think?"

"Nice." I fingered the slippery fabric. The dress had a midriff cutout the size of a ship porthole. "But it's pretty daring. Are you really going to wear it?"

"No." Selfie's eyes sparkled. *"You are."*

I blinked in amazement. Then I heard my mother's voice in my head: "Becca, what in the world are you *wearing*?"

I shook my head. "It's—really cool, but . . . do you have anything, uh, less . . ." *Totally unlike me?*

Selfie returned with more options.

I shook my head at each one. Finally, Selfie produced a simple white shift with tiny stars. I didn't want to get undressed in front of her, so I pulled the dress on over my shirt.

"It's perfect," I said, admiring myself in the mirror. "But it's about two feet too long."

"That's what tailors are for," Selfie said, picking up a phone. "Olga, could you come down? Thanks."

I had no idea who Olga was, but I wanted to know more about Selfie's date. "So what are your plans with Jean-Luc? Are you going out to dinner first?"

"Nope." Selfie swiped her phone. "We're meeting at the dance. He's flying straight in from his soccer game."

That didn't follow the script. As I'd learned from Selfie, the pre-prom routine involved an exchange of corsages, a photo session with ten best friends, and a limo ride. But if Selfie didn't care, good for her.

"Ooh! He sent another pic." Selfie's face lit up, and she handed me the phone. "Pretty gorge, huh?"

I nodded. Was he really only fourteen? Truthfully, he was almost *too* good-looking, with his tanned skin and sun-streaked hair. Even his friends were handsome.

"Have you *talked* to him?" It suddenly occurred to me she hadn't.

"That part of the Alps doesn't get good cell reception."

Someone knocked. "Come in," Selfie yelled, still absorbed in her phone. A maid in a uniform set down a pitcher of lemonade filled with lemon slices, and a plate of cupcakes and other treats.

She smiled. "We have salted caramel, chocolate mint, and red velvet. Hand-churned gelato and homemade whoopie pies. Gourmet ice pops in key lime pie, cherry hibiscus, and cotton candy."

"Thanks, Clara." Selfie took a glass of lemonade and a whoopie pie. Clara started straightening magazines.

"So how well did you know Jean-Luc at camp?" I asked.

She picked a thread off her shirt. "Oh, you know. Not *really* well, but ..."

I hesitated. "But you do *remember* him, right?"

Selfie shrugged and sipped her drink. "Well ... yes and no."

I felt a hitch of surprise.

"Yes and *no*?" I repeated. "What does that—"

The door opened again, and suddenly, a tall woman with a measuring tape around her neck was standing in front of us. She cleared her throat.

"Hi, Olga," said Selfie. "Becca needs alterations."

The tall woman looked me up and down, frowning. "This is the girl?" *Even she can't believe we're friends.*

While Olga measured me, a handsome thirtyish man with a headset walked through the open door. Dressed in khakis and a polo shirt, he held out his hand to shake. "I'm Brendan, Mrs. St. Claire's assistant."

Now there were *three* staff people in the room. No wonder Selfie couldn't get any homework done.

"Hi." I shook Brendan's hand, while trying to stand still for Olga. "I'm Becca."

"Welcome." His smile was charming. "I'm glad Clara set you up with snacks. Would you like a tour?" He turned to Selfie. "I can show her the Matisse, the glass elevator, and the zoo. The baby llama has a feeding in five minutes."

My heart bounced. "Awesome!"

Olga finished up, and rolled up her tape measure.

"Go!" Selfie blew me a kiss. "I have to leave for a museum benefit."

"Uh, okay—" I let Brendan lead me out of the room. I still had a bunch of questions about Jean-Luc, but I figured I'd get to them later. As it turned out, though, the next few days were so jammed with chores, studying, and prom prep, I never followed up.

Worst.

Mistake.

Ever.

Chapter 13

"He's he-ere!" my mother shouted from downstairs. Dinesh was outside to pick me up for prom.

In my bedroom, I took one last look in the mirror. I barely recognized me.

My hands shook as I came downstairs. School dances, rides with boys, and other grown-up adventures—it was all starting now. No more clothes from Children's World ("From Tots to Teens, and In Between"). Trying new things—even if Rosa and Prezbo disapproved.

"You look beautiful, sweetheart." My mother smoothed my hair and called to my father,

"Sam, come see your grown-up daughter."

My dad blinked a few times when he saw me. We were all trying to play it cool, as if a strange boy picking me up wasn't an earth-shaking event in our house.

Ding-dong. Ding-dong. Ding—

I opened the door. Dinesh looked so handsome, I actually jumped back a bit. He wore a tweed jacket, blue shirt, and dark tie. His wild black hair fell over his forehead. I tried to smile at him, but he wouldn't meet my eyes.

He's nervous, too, I thought.

My mom smiled warmly. "Hi, Dinesh. I'm Jill; this is Sam. Come in!"

"Uh, okay." Dinesh glanced back at the car. "For a minute."

My dad led us into the living room and held up his camera. "I thought we'd take pictures here."

Dinesh looked at his watch.

"Stand closer together." My dad moved around, shooting from different angles.

I felt Dinesh's impatience.

"So you'll come right home afterward?" My mom lifted her eyebrow.

I shot her an exasperated look.

"Straightaway," Dinesh assured her, then headed out the door.

I followed, a little disappointed Dinesh hadn't seemed to notice my dazzling prom getup. Not even a "You look nice!" or "Cool dress." Jean-Luc would probably gasp when he saw Selfie in her prom outfit and say a lot of romantic things in French.

My mom waved from the doorway. I was glad she didn't come outside. I didn't want to squirm while she asked the driver—probably Dinesh's mom—a million questions.

I climbed into the SUV. "Oh!" I gasped, as seven pairs of eyes stared back at me. No wonder Dinesh looked so uncomfortable taking pictures at my house— half the seventh grade was waiting in the car.

"Carpooling saves gas," Dinesh said, without a smile. "Sit down." He pointed to the back row, while he took a seat near the front. He was as far from me as he could be and still be in the car.

A teenage guy with glasses in the driver's seat turned around. "Hi, I'm Kabir, Dinesh's brother. And you are . . . ?"

"Becca," I said, confused by Dinesh's coldness.

"What *grade* are you?" Jamiah Page demanded.

"Sixth," I said, and she frowned.

Looking around, I recognized a few people. Mandy Griswold. Corey Strohmer. They were smart seventh graders who were in jazz band, Eco-Teens, and Hooked on Books. They were the kind of people I would have liked to get to know, but they all had their backs turned.

"—still thinks *blogs* are cool—"

"—crushing it in hacky-sack—"

"—K-pop—"

I waited for an opening. Even though I had more in common with this group than Selfie's crowd, they felt just as off-limits. I tried to catch Dinesh's eye.

He wouldn't look at me.

Weird, but—maybe I was imagining things. Determined to join in, I called out to Dinesh from the back seat. "Hey, Dinesh, uh, do you know who the band is tonight?"

"HUH?"

Dinesh turned around, startled. "Uh, sorry, I . . ." He bolted out of the car as soon as it pulled into a driveway. My shoulders slumped. Now there was no denying it: *Something was up.*

The SUV door opened again, and Anders Cho climbed in, a cool, brainy guy wearing a Western-style bolo tie, probably as a joke. To make room for him, I

crawled into the tiny way-back seat. No one was talking to me anyway. *For this I blew off Rosa and Prezbo?*

"Oh, Anders!" Some girls were laughing.

Numb with misery, I slumped in the corner. I cleared aside junk on the seat—magazines, candy wrappers, ballpoint pens.

Looking out the window, my mood got even darker. Dinesh had been acting strange from the second he'd picked me up. The question was *why*. Was he embarrassed by my dad's picture taking? Had he finally realized how nerdy and out of it I was? Could he tell how much I liked him? Tears swelled behind my eyes, threatening to spill.

No way we're going to dance together now.

Prom was horrible, and it hadn't even begun yet.

STOP, I ordered myself. *Think about something else.* I grabbed a teen fashion magazine off the floor. Flipping through random pages, I saw a feature on Fashion Week. A perfume ad. A movie premiere. Young skiers drinking hot chocolate.

Hot chocolate?

Wait a minute ... HOLY FREAKIN' CRUD.

It was Jean-Luc.

Selfie had showed me Jean-Luc's picture. Now, here it was again . . . *in an ad for fancy watches.*

My brain was exploding. No wonder the photo had looked so professional, and his buddies so handsome. It was an ad! These kids were models, not a group of friends. Jean-Luc was made-up!

So now the question was:

Who was lying to Selfie?

She had to be warned.

IMMEDIATELY.

If Selfie got to the dance before I reached her, she was dead. I knew *Action News* anchor Rob Robson would be holding "red carpet" interviews, like on the Oscars, and there'd be no bigger "get" than Selfie.

I had to stop her before she bragged about a date that didn't exist.

But she wasn't picking up her phone. In the back of Dinesh's car, I frantically redialed.

"Selfie here. Leave me a message." (*BEEP*)

I tapped again.

"Selfie here. Leave me a message." (*BEEP*)

Again.

"Selfie here. Leave—"

She was probably getting out of her limo right around now. I imagined the chauffeur laying a fur wrap on her shoulders while Selfie smiled and waved at the crowd.

"Oh, Di-*nesh*!" Maya teased from the middle seat. He flashed a crooked smile. *GET ME OUT OF HERE!*

Meanwhile, I was replaying my last conversation with Selfie. *We're meeting at the dance. That part of the Alps doesn't get good phone reception.* How had I missed the signals?

Who was mean enough to invent a phony prom date? I had a pretty good guess.

Roxxi.

She lived to embarrass Selfie, while pretending to defend her. She got jealous when people talked about Selfie's latest scandal, boyfriend, or new satin boxer shorts. But would even *Roxxi* pull such an evil prank?

Hurry, hurry, I silently begged Kabir. Finally, I couldn't hold back.

"Are we, uh, almost there?" my voice squeaked from the backseat.

"Why?" Anders turned around. "Hot date?"

Everyone laughed.

Just when I thought I couldn't take another second, Kabir swung into the parking lot. I leaped out of the car like it was in flames and raced toward the school building.

People flooded around the entrance. As I got closer, I caught a glimpse of the red carpet—really a rubber mat—and saw giant lights and a camera. Rob was in the middle of the crowd, talking to someone I couldn't see. *Please don't let it be Selfie!*

But it was too late.

" . . . flying in for a top-level soccer tournament." Selfie's face was glowing. "He'll be here any minute."

Don't say more! I wanted to shout. I wondered how I could stop the interview—faint, make a scene, pull a fire alarm?

The crowd watched Selfie with envy. As usual, she appeared to have it made—wearing a knockout dress, doing a VIP interview, describing a super-cool date. Her life looked perfect.

I checked out the rest of the glam crowd. Roxxi was dragging around a tall, shaggy-haired guy who was absorbed in his phone. D'Nise was stepping out of a long white car with a boy in an old-fashioned gangster suit with big shoulders. Vivienne and Chaz wore matching tuxes with yellow-rose boutonnieres.

Maybe I had been too quick to focus on Roxxi. Any of them could have invented Jean-Luc.

I studied them all.

"So is this guy famous?" Rob asked Selfie. "Have we heard of him?"

Oh boy.

"Most Americans don't know junior European soccer stars," Selfie said, avoiding the question like a politician.

I glanced at Roxxi. She was listening to the interview with a little smile. Did she know something . . . or was she just being polite?

"Where'd you meet?" Rob asked.

"Swiss summer camp." Selfie looked around.

"You must be stoked for the Dude 'n' Diva Awards. People say you're the favorite," Rob confided. "What do *you* think?"

"I think it's time to get some punch."

With Queen Bee confidence, she sailed off toward the gym, swinging a stylish evening bag. I practically tackled her.

"Oof!" She grunted as I dragged her to the side. "Careful, Becca!" She smoothed her dress. "You're going to tear the crystals off!"

"Listen—"

"Let me look at you!" She scanned me up and down. "Adorbs! You just need a dab of lip shine. Here, I'll—"

I wriggled away. "We have an emergency."

"Your makeup's *fine*—"

Tears sprang to my eyes.

"Becca." Selfie blinked. "What *is* it?"

"It's about Jean-Luc." I swallowed. I took a deep breath. How do you tell someone they're about to be publicly humiliated?

"He doesn't exist," I choked out.

"W-What?"

"He's *made-up*. Invented. You know that photo of the ski crowd?" I showed her the torn-out magazine page. "It's from an ad. I saw it in *Teen Vogue*."

Selfie grabbed the page. Strange, whimpering sounds came from the back of her throat.

"*There is no Jean-Luc*," I said.

Just then, we heard a voice behind us.

"*Mademoiselle...?*"

Selfie and I slowly turned around....

Chapter 14

In front of us was a short, strangely dressed guy with a hat worn low over his face. Sunglasses hid his eyes, and a silk scarf was twisted around his neck.

"*Allo*," he said. "I am Jean-Luc."

Our jaws dropped.

"Jean-Luc?" I repeated dumbly. He nodded. Apparently, he *wasn't* made-up.

Selfie just stared.

"But—you don't look like your picture!" I took out the magazine ad. Unlike the hunky guy in the photo, Jean-Luc was short, looked about eleven, and did NOT have a ski tan.

"Well . . ." He shrugged. "'Ere I am."

This guy was seriously off. Not only was his photo a lie, but his French accent wasn't very . . . *French. Who was he?*

Prom-goers walked by us toward the school entrance. Selfie pulled Jean-Luc around the corner, next to a sports equipment shed.

"Take your sunglasses off," Selfie ordered.

Jean-Luc shook his head.

"*And* the hat. *And* the scarf."

He didn't move.

"*NOW.*"

He took his time unraveling the scarf, which was printed with tiny squirrels. He unbuttoned his raincoat. Off came his hat, revealing curly dark hair. Finally, he took off his glasses.

Selfie and I gasped.

"FELIX!"

Jean-Luc was Felix Needleman, the sixth-grade geek with a fierce unibrow. *Felix Needleman!* I remembered him staring at Selfie in the Multi-Purpose Room, when we'd met with Dinesh. Selfie had totally ignored him.

Now he was her *prom date*?

I backed Felix against the wall. "Start talking."

Selfie stood in her fur wrap with her high heels apart, glaring.

"First I followed her on Instagram," he explained. "To see what she liked."

"Go on," I said through gritted teeth.

"I saw pics from Swiss summer camp. So . . ." A note of pride crept into his voice. "I created Jean-Luc. A rich French guy."

"I really, *really*, don't believe this," said Selfie, rubbing her forehead.

"I worked at it. I watched a reality show about an Italian prince. Read up on foreign sports cars."

I groaned. "And then?"

He shrugged. "The e-mails just kind of wrote themselves."

"So you think you did a great job, huh?" I shook with anger. "Well, you ruined prom. And maybe *her life*."

With that, Selfie burst into tears.

Oh *no*. I didn't mean to make her feel worse! Now mascara was running down her face in jagged stripes. I sat down next to her and patted her back. But her fur wrap kept filling up with big, wet blotches.

Looking scared, Felix sat down, too. "I'm—I'm sorry. Hearing back from her was . . ." He sighed. "*Amazing*. Once it started, I couldn't give it up."

I felt a weird pang of sympathy for him, which I tried to resist. "What did you *think* would happen when she found out you lied?"

"I figured she'd be surprised at first. But when she got to know me, she'd be impressed."

"UGGH!" Selfie made a noise that was either a sob or a snort.

This guy!

"That day in the Multi-Purpose Room, she wouldn't even *talk* to me," Felix explained. "It was like I was invisible."

Unfortunately, I could relate.

"If I can just get one date with her, I thought. I'll show her I'm not just a gaming freak. I know movie trivia. I do comedy routines." He leaned over, confiding. "You should see my Mr. Krabs."

For a geeky sixth grader, he had a lot of confidence. In spite of myself, I was sort of impressed.

"I just wanted a shot," he said sadly. "Everyone deserves a shot."

Selfie turned to him with blazing eyes.

"Not on *prom night*."

She ran off, sobbing.

I went after Selfie, leaving Felix alone on the concrete bench. I felt horrible for her. There was no handbook for this.

Where *was* she? I looked around, but the night was dense, black, and foggy. Most people were streaming toward school, which was lit up like a cruise ship. I went in the opposite direction, figuring Selfie might go toward the parking lot. As people came toward me, I swerved around them, until . . .

THWOK!

I bumped into someone.

Oh, crud.

We stood there awkwardly. "Where are you going?" he asked, since I was walking against the tide of prom guests.

I sighed. "Long story."

Both of us looked at the ground.

"Is this about . . ." He swallowed. "Felix?"

I looked up. I had forgotten they were friends. Then suddenly, it hit me. "You *knew*! You knew all about—"

"NO!"

I looked at him.

"I mean—" He took a deep breath. "I only found out tonight, right before I saw you. H-He swore me to secrecy!" His eyes were frantic. "That's why I acted weird in the car—I didn't know what to say."

No wonder he wouldn't look at me.

Dinesh shook his head. "I wish he *had* told me before. I would have stopped him! What an *idiot*."

Relief washed over me. Dinesh seemed as upset with Felix as I was.

"Where *is* Felix?" He glanced around.

"I just left him." I pointed backward. "I'm looking for Selfie."

"How did she react?" he hesitated. "Bit upset, I take it?"

I nodded. "It was pretty bad."

We were both quiet, hearing music coming from the gym.

"Felix is probably pretty messed up right now," said Dinesh. "I better find him. Make sure he's all right."

"Yeah, I've got to go help Selfie," I said, not moving.

"It's too bad we won't get to . . ." He looked at the ground.

I waited.

"You know. Have a dance together."

Hearing him say it out loud made my spine tingle.

He started off toward Felix, then he turned back. "Unless . . . you can think of some way to fix this?"

It seemed pretty unfixable. But my dance with Dinesh—and all my dreams—depended on it.

· · ● · ·

"We have two options," I told Selfie. After I left Dinesh, I'd found her slumped against a tree near the parking lot. Prom was in full swing—we had to make a decision, fast.

"Number one, we make up a story," I continued.

"His plane got delayed. Soccer injury. Yacht accident. *Whatever.*"

"No one'll believe it," said Selfie. "What's number two?"

I took a deep breath.

"We pass Felix off as your date."

"WHAT?"

"For *ten minutes*! Just long enough to show you had one." My eyes locked with hers.

"He's a foot shorter than me," she said quietly.

"So? Some French guys are short." I shrugged. "The gym will be dark. He'll be covered up. You make a little small talk, you wave, and move on. Then we get him out—quickly.

"And remember, he's a sixth grader," I added. "Half these people don't even know him."

Selfie was silent a moment. "You really think he can pull this off?"

I smiled. "He was smart enough to fool *us*, wasn't he?"

After a scolding from Dinesh, Felix seemed eager to help Selfie save face. I explained the plan. With a dose of luck, we might—*might*—pull it off. I went ahead to scope out the situation.

When I walked into prom, I gasped.

Our grubby gym had been transformed into an elegant ballroom. The tables were covered with shiny gold silk. White tulle billowed from the ceiling. There were tinsel chandeliers and giant flower arrangements. Guests entered through an archway of silver balloons, past a silhouette of the New York City skyline.

But I wondered: Why was the dance floor empty? After a jarring drum solo, I knew why. In an effort to be "sophisticated," the Dance Committee had hired an ultramodern free-jazz quartet.

Unfortunately, their music was totally un-danceable.

Off the dance floor, people stood around stiffly, sipping "mocktails"—club soda with orange juice and lime wedges. Girls inspected one another's dresses, while boys tugged at their collars, looking uncomfortable. Instead of talking, people checked their phones.

Weird.

Roxxi passed by and inspected my dress. "Looks like you finally discovered the teen department," she sniffed.

"Where's Selfie? I'm dying to see her date," said Clementine. The prom guru and school's biggest gossip was sitting at the entrance table.

"You'll see them," I promised.

"She's got to sign the guest book," Clem said, pointing at the fancy album in front of her.

Clem was the key to our plan. If Clem spotted "Jean-Luc," she'd spread it all over school: *Selfie had a date. I saw him.* The trick was to give her a distant glance, not a face-to-face meeting.

Luckily, the "romantic" lighting made it hard to see. At the far end of the gym was a forest of white branches, draped in tiny fairy lights. Selfie and Felix could hide there, come out, and wave. I'd make sure Clem saw them—and then we'd make our escape.

Selfie and Felix sneaked behind the building, through the rear gym door, and slipped into the Enchanted Forest. Dinesh and I stepped behind Clem.

"Wow, there's Selfie and her date!" called out Dinesh.

Clem looked up eagerly.

"The guy in the weird hat?" Clem squinted. "I can barely see him."

Across the gym, we saw Felix and Selfie, but his face was in the shadows. Selfie forced a smile and waved.

YES!

"They make a cute couple," said Dinesh, winking at me.

Selfie and Felix ducked behind a tree, but Clem had seen enough to know Selfie was with someone. News would get around—*fast.* Our crazy plan was working.

"Sushi's here!" someone shouted, and men in white jackets carried out silver trays. Each tray had elaborate food sculptures made of eel and octopus, arranged in the shape of a different world landmark: the Eiffel Tower, the Empire State Building, the Taj Mahal. Impressive, but they seemed better to look at than to eat.

I ran into the Enchanted Forest to congratulate Selfie and Felix. "We did it!" I gave them a thumbs-up. "Clem saw you for one second. It was perfect!"

Selfie sighed. "*That's* a relief."

We were just about to slip out the back when . . .

"*There* you are!"

Even before I spun around, I knew it was Roxxi.

"You must be Jean-Luc!" she said, swooping in for a Euro-style double kiss. "Fabulous to meet you."

Startled, he wiped his face.

"What school do you go to?" Roxxi asked excitedly. "The International School? Le Rosey?"

"A small, uh, *académie.*" He coughed. "Of science." He pronounced it like "se-ance."

"What is this, an interview?" Selfie joked. "We have to—"

Roxxi ignored her, taking Felix's arm like they were old friends. "And you play ... *soccer*? What position?"

Felix looked scared.

"Uh ... forward. Backward. Jump guard."

Roxxi looked skeptical. Selfie stepped between them. "We have to go."

"Hold on." Roxxi pushed Selfie aside again. "Tell me more. What other activities do you like?"

"Ahhh ..." He bit his lip. "Sled polo. Racing of large dogs. Heli-skating."

Roxxi frowned. *"What?"*

Suddenly, Rob Robson's voice boomed over the mic. "Ladies and gentlemen, it's that time you've been waiting for . . . the DUDE 'N' DIVA AWARDS!"

The dance floor filled up instantly as everyone swarmed to hear who'd won. Roxxi looked torn, but finally moved toward Rob.

"This is our chance!" I whispered.

Rob blathered on about the contest and what a great tradition it was, *blah, blah, blah*. Once he got hold of a mic, he couldn't let go. Selfie, Felix, and I tiptoed toward the door, staying against the wall.

Step by step. We passed the glittering Manhattan skyline. That meant we were close.

A few people glanced at us, but it didn't matter. The door was seconds away.

Three, two . . .

"And the winners are . . ."

One . . .

"SLOAN ST. CLAIRE and JEAN-LUC GIRARD!"

Selfie and Felix froze. A spotlight swung around and caught them in a blinding glare.

Oh, *crud*.

Chapter 15

"Bring the happy couple up for a dance!" Rob shouted. Everyone whistled and applauded.

Selfie turned ghostly white.

Felix broke into a smile, but he saw Selfie's reaction and stopped.

"*Go* Selfie. *Go* Selfie. *Go*—" people chanted.

She just stood there, stunned, until Felix led her to the dance floor. People surrounded them, eager to check out her famous date. I swallowed. *How long before someone recognizes him?*

The musicians struck up another un-danceable tune. I edged along the wall for a better view. Selfie

smiled through gritted teeth. She pulled his head into her neck to hide his face, and they began a slow, awkward dance.

Finally, it ended.

"Let's all join them on the dance floor," Rob urged. The band struck up a fast song, but no one moved. Watching the unusual couple was much too interesting. Selfie tried to pull away, but Felix was just getting started.

To everyone's amazement, Felix knew how to dance. After a blizzard of fancy footwork, he took Selfie's hand and twirled her around. She looked startled, but the audience loved his old-school dance steps. He twirled her again.

"Ooohs" rippled through the gym.

I could see Selfie whispering to Felix, probably asking him to cool it. But his moves got even wilder.

Hoots, whistles, cheers.

Feeding off the crowd's energy, he swept her into a dramatic dip. Everyone held up their phones to film it.

"Kiss her!" someone yelled.

Felix seemed to consider it. His mouth and Selfie's were inches apart. Selfie's eyes widened in horror as the drumbeat got louder.

"KISS! KISS! KISS!"

Felix's lips moved even closer, and he gave her a big kiss.

Sma-a-a-ack!

"OOOOOOOHHHHH!!!" The room went nuts.

Selfie pushed him away. "KNOCK IT OFF!" Felix started to apologize, but she said, "I'm done." And

then she reached over and tore off Felix's hat and glasses.

The sight of Felix's curly hair and unibrow brought gasps of disbelief.

"Is that ... ?"

"NAAAW!"

"Felix Needleman!??"

Giggles and whispers rocked the room. Selfie grabbed Rob's mic.

"Well, now you know," she said flatly. She pointed to a startled Felix. "His name isn't 'Jean-Luc.' He's not French, and he doesn't play soccer. He goes to *magic camp*."

Felix added, "I'm also a champion Lego—"

Selfie held up a finger. "What I'm trying to say is, this whole prom thing's gotten out of hand. I wanted a date so bad, I ended up with a fake-French sixth grader. And I can't even be mad at him for lying, cuz . . ." She swallowed. "I lied, too."

The audience leaned in.

"I told everyone I had this amazing date lined up." Selfie sighed. "But I didn't have *anyone*. And I let the lie get bigger and bigger. That's how much I wanted to crush prom."

Everyone's eyes widened.

"Now I realize . . ." Selfie shook her head sadly. "I was missing the whole point. Why do we have prom, anyway? It should be to have fun, not to impress people."

"What does *that* mean?" Roxxi asked sharply.

"Look at this party." Selfie's eyes swept the room. "We have fancy food no one likes. A band we can't

dance to. Clothes we can't wait to change out of." She sighed. "Why are we all pretending we're in *high school*? Is anyone—*really*—having fun?"

This was huge. The most popular girl in school had just admitted she wasn't enjoying prom. I looked around.

The room was deadly quiet.

Finally, Margaux Frost broke the silence. "These heels are so high, I can hardly walk."

"This tux cost a year's allowance," said a beefy jock.

"This food is weird." Clem pulled seaweed out of her teeth.

"My date is actually my cousin," Roxxi admitted.

"I had to bribe mine with an Xbox One," D'Nise said quietly.

People were coming up and patting Selfie on the shoulder, confiding their own disasters. The color was back in her cheeks. Maybe admitting the truth had made her feel good about herself again. Judging from the crowd around her, it seemed to have made her even *more* popular.

People circled Felix, too. "I learned those spins from old movies," he explained. "It was fun, but I'm zonked out. BTW, does this dance have an eyeglass repair station?"

"There you are!" Dinesh came up to me. Just then, my phone buzzed. It was a text from Rosa.

HELP!!!!

Uh-oh.

"I've got to go to MORP!" I shouted to Dinesh over the noise.

"I'll come, too," he said. "Felix doesn't need me anymore."

I broke into a run, with Dinesh close behind. I had to rescue Rosa and Prezbo, even if one of them wasn't speaking to me.

We stepped through the basement door into Morp. The first thing I noticed was the smell.

A guy in high-tech headphones ran up to me. "*Please* say you're delivering a pizza," he begged.

"Sorry." I shrugged.

The atmosphere in the basement was glum. A few tech nerds leaned on crates of toilet paper, rolling twelve-sided dice. Goth girls glared at us from their perch on a discarded air conditioner. A guy in a biohazard suit sat alone, playing games on his phone. The fluorescent lights gave the room a cold green glow.

Dinesh drifted away, and I scanned the room for Prezbo. He was next to the sink, handing out cans of soda. His face lit up when he saw me, then turned uncertain. I was unsure, too. Neither of us budged. I walked away, feeling sad.

Rosa bolted over to me.

"What took you so long . . . ?" she started to complain, then her eyes widened at my fancy outfit. *"Holy crud."*

I folded my arms, trying to hide my filmy dress. By contrast, she was dressed to work at a car wash.

"Are you wearing . . . *eye makeup*!?" she asked, astounded. I shrugged, feeling embarrassed.

"Well?" Rosa looked around. "What do you think of MORP?"

I stalled for time. "It's—wow. The place looks . . . uh . . ." *Say something.* "Great idea, covering the walls with graffiti."

"The graffiti was already there," said Rosa flatly.

"Oh." *Oops.*

She explained her idea of Morp to Dinesh. "We wanted it super chill," she said. "No dumb 'planned' activities. Just, do what you want to do." She squashed a cockroach with her hiking boot. "Why obsess over every detail?"

You could have obsessed a little more, I thought. They were so busy rebelling against prom, they'd made their event a little *too* un-special. I liked the quirky spirit, but it barely seemed like a party at all.

Blaze, the graffiti artist, tapped Rosa on the shoulder. "We need more paper. We work large, ya know?" His crew surrounded her, impatient.

Before Rosa could answer, a girl with a ukulele tugged her sleeve. "How can we have a 'jam session' if we don't know the same songs?" She pointed to a guy holding a trombone.

A mob formed around Rosa, shouting complaints.

"You said there'd be dancing!"

"Where's the ice?"

"The Scrabble set only has one *F*!"

"You *said*—"

"You *promised*—"

Rosa spun around, frantic. "PREZBO!"

The party was about to self-destruct. *Why oh why
didn't I help Rosa and Prezbo more?* If I hadn't been
so caught up with Selfie, I could have hung chili pep-
per lights and brought two-bite brownies. I'd have
pushed for a deejay. Now it was too late.

Above the shouting, I heard the door creak open.

"So *this* is Morp . . . ?"

Selfie and her friends were standing there.

The Morpers looked stunned as the room filled up
with poofy dresses, tuxedos, and towering updos.
Purse chains jangled. Silk rustled.

The prom kids squirmed. They'd probably expected to blend into a noisy party, not be stared at
like criminals. The room fell into an awkward
silence.

Rosa's voice was blunt. "Why aren't you at prom?"

Selfie stepped forward.

"Actually . . . ?" She shrugged. "Prom was kind of . . . *ehhh*."

Oh? I could feel the Morpers' ears prick up.

"At least we had *music*," a prom guy muttered.

"So go back!" a goth girl snapped.

Nobody moved. It was a standoff.

Then someone dropped a Ping-Pong ball.

We all watched dumbly as it bounced on the floor, rolled under a table, hit a pipe, popped up over a bench, and landed in a janitor's bucket. Elvin, a skinny Morper, came forward and scooped it up, embarrassed.

"Bet you couldn't do that again," snorted Zach Pirotta.

"Oh yeah? Bet I could," said Elvin. Everyone watched as he took aim and carefully tossed it. It bounced, rolled, jumped, and just *barely* missed going into the bucket.

"My turn!" called Zach.

"Let's make it harder," said Felix, popping up out of nowhere. He and some guys gathered paint cans, mop handles, and paper cups to beef up the obstacle course. A couple people scoffed or raised their eyebrows as if to say, *What are these nerds doing?*

The course took shape.

And suddenly, the game was on. People crowded around to take a turn. Every kid there—jocks, skate punks, Harry Potter freaks—wanted to play.

Something in the room changed. Tuxedo jackets were removed. Rules were debated. Bets were placed. As the border between prom and Morp dissolved, people scattered to play mini-golf, skim the comic book rack, or check out the weird mold on the ceiling.

At the graffiti wall, Vivienne and Margaux stood next to Blaze, drawing hearts and smileys between the burning skulls and cartoon gangster animals.

There were other strange sights, too. At the bandstand, D'Nise was belting out a rap song. Behind her was Ukulele Girl, the electric guitar guys, a girl on bongos, and Ajax, beatboxing. They were being led

by—*of all people*—the sax player from prom's snooty jazz band.

The cracked cement dance floor was crammed. The prom girls were holding each other and swaying, while the goth kids did a crazy, punk dance.

The noise made Luther, the security guard, stomp downstairs. "I WILL SHUT THIS THING *DOWN*, PEOPLE!" he thundered. Everyone froze. Then his eyes strayed to a candy bowl. "Are those . . . *gummy sharks*?"

It was starting to look like a party.

I glanced over at Prezbo, who was spraying Cheese Whiz on crackers. He must have known I was there, but he wouldn't look at me. My heart felt as heavy as a brick. Was this the new "normal"?

No freakin' way. If he couldn't do it, I would. Taking a deep breath, I walked up to him.

"Hey." I looked around. "Can you believe this?"

Prezbo put down the cheese can.

"I know." He half snorted.

"How does it feel to throw a party that's wildly popular?"

"It's . . ." He looked thoughtful. "Weird. I'm

usually suspicious of anything popular."

We both laughed.

He waited a beat. "How was prom?"

Big question. "Over-the-top. Embarrassing. Tons of drama. Exactly what I wanted." I smiled.

He smiled back. I laughed again. Maybe we weren't so far apart after all.

"Prez, I have to go find Selfie and Dinesh." I watched for a reaction, but he just nodded and waved. "But I'll be back." And I meant it.

I found Dinesh negotiating with the ragged group of musicians, which included members of the jazz quartet. "Hey, Becca," he greeted me. "I'm just trying to get these guys to take a request. Remember, I owe you a dance."

"Oh! Right."

As if I could forget!

Dinesh whispered something to the band-leader, and they struck up a song that was slow, dreamy, and old-fashioned. Loud complaining followed, with shouts of "Uggghh!" and people stomping off the tiny dance floor. Dinesh stepped onto it and reached out his hand to me.

I leaned into him and inhaled, wanting to drink in every detail of my first dance with a boy. *Ahhhhh.* He smelled like deodorant soap and old library books. A jazz guy crooned . . .

"*Birds singing in the sycamore tree*
Dream a little dream of me."

Not knowing how to dance, we kind of shuffled in place, only occasionally coinciding with the music. "Crazy night," he muttered under his breath. I nodded, feeling his heartbeat.

"Booo!" "Yuck!" "Bring back rap!" people yelled.

The jazz guys stopped playing to argue with the protesters. After a shouting match, the band switched to a song known for pumping up crowds at sports stadiums. Our dance was over.

"Oh well." Dinesh shrugged. "We tried." And then he smiled his crooked smile. "I'm going to grab a vegan s'more."

Disappointment washed over me, but I forced a smile. *Why can't we finish our dance?* My cheek still had the imprint of his jacket on it. I cursed the noisy mob on the dance floor. We were robbed.

Still, how upset could I be? I'd gotten to dance with *Dinesh O'Reilly*. That was crazy. I'd replay the moment over and over. Would we ever hang out again? Maybe not—but it didn't even matter. Tonight, I had a dream come true.

Now I had to find Selfie. I finally spotted her playing School Basement Mini-Golf. She was deep in conversation with Felix.

Felix?

"Put some spin on it," he urged as Selfie took aim.

"You guys are getting along?" I blurted.

Selfie shrugged. "He apologized. Besides, he's teaching me how to play."

"By Grabthar's hammer, by the sons of Warvan, you shall be avenged!" said Felix. "*Galaxy Quest*," he added.

"He's pretty funny," Selfie said, smiling. "Maybe not as funny as he *thinks* he is, but . . ."

She started taking off her shoes. All around us, other prom-goers were eagerly removing high heels or unstrapping sandals.

As if they were planning to stay awhile.

I pulled Selfie aside.

"I liked what you said at the mic tonight," I said. "I liked it a lot."

Selfie's smile deepened. "Good. Cuz I got it from *you*."

"*Me?*"

"Remember? You said I shouldn't worry what other people think. To go have fun whether I had a date or not."

I stood there staring.

"I forgot the exact words." Selfie hesitated. "I hope I said it right."

Too choked up to speak, I nodded.

"Nothing worked out tonight." She shook her head. "But—somehow—I'm okay with it."

"Me too."

Who needed perfection? I was happy with half a dance, a laugh with Prezbo, and a diva who remembered what I'd said to her.

"Want to dance?" she asked.

I smiled.

Acknowledgments
With Love and thanks to David

Thank you for reading this Feiwel & Friends book.
The friends who made

THIS DANCE IS
DOOMED

possible are:

Jean Feiwel, *Publisher*

Liz Szabla, *Associate Publisher*

Rich Deas, *Senior Creative Director*

Holly West, *Senior Editor*

Anna Roberto, *Senior Editor*

Kat Brzozowski, *Senior Editor*

Dawn Ryan, *Senior Managing Editor*

Kim Waymer, *Senior Production Manager*

Emily Settle, *Associate Editor*

Erin Siu, *Associate Editor*

Rachel Diebel, *Assistant Editor*

Foyinsi Adegbonmire, *Editorial Assistant*

Trisha Previte, *Designer*

Starr Baer, *Associate Copy Chief*

Follow us on Facebook or visit us
online at mackids.com.
Our books are friends for life.